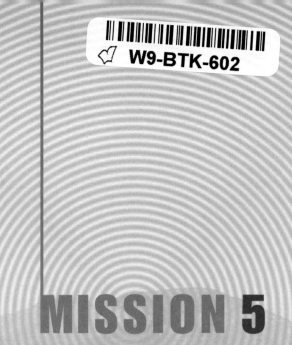

MISSION 5

SOLE SURVIVOR

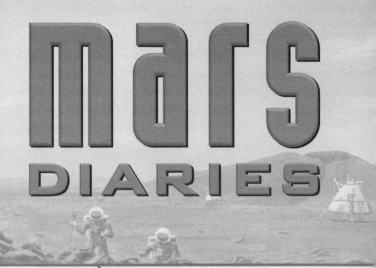

MARS DIARIES

MISSION 5

SOLE SURVIVOR

SIGMUND BROUWER

TYNDALE HOUSE PUBLISHERS, INC.
WHEATON, ILLINOIS

Visit Tyndale's exciting Web site at www.tyndale.com

You can contact Sigmund Brouwer through his Web site at
www.coolreading.com

Designed by Beth Sparkman

Edited by Ramona Cramer Tucker

Scripture quotations are taken from the *Holy Bible,* New Living Translation,
copyright © 1996. Used by permission of Tyndale House Publishers, Inc.,
Wheaton, Illinois 60189. All rights reserved.

ISBN 0-8423-4308-3

Printed in the United States of America

07   06   05   04   03   02   01
7   6   5   4   3   2   1

CHAPTER 1

Cave-in!

The wheels of the robot body under my control hummed as the robot sped across the red, packed sands of the flat valley floor toward the hills about five miles from the dome.

Thin Martian wind whistled around me, picking up the grains of sand that the robot wheels sent flying into the air. The sky was butterscotch colored, the sun a perfect circle of blue. Thin streaks of light blue clouds hung above the distant mountain peaks.

But I wasn't about to spend any energy appreciating the beauty of the Martian landscape.

Not with a cave-in ahead and desperate scientists waiting for whatever rescue attempt was possible. Robot bodies don't sweat with fear. But if they did, my own fear would have beaded on the shiny surface of the robot's titanium shell. While I was still in the dome, on a laboratory bed using X-ray waves to direct the robot body, all my thoughts were frantic with total fear and worry.

Once before I'd been sent on a rescue mission. A real rescue mission, instead of the usual virtual-reality tests for the robot body that I'd spent years learning to handle as if it were my own body. The first rescue mission had been to search for only one person, lost in the cornfields of the science station's greenhouse.

This time was just as real.

And far more frightening.

Two hours earlier, four people in space suits had walked into a cave to take rock samples. They were searching for traces of ancient water activity and fossil bacteria. According to standard field procedure, they'd sent back their activities on real-time video transmissions beamed directly to the dome. An hour later—only 60 minutes ago—the images and their voices had stopped abruptly, thrown into blackness and drowned out by a horrible rumbling that could only be caused by the collapse of the cave's ceiling. Now all that remained to give an indication of their location deep inside the rock were the signals thrown by the g.p.u. in each of their space suits—a global positioning unit that bounced sound waves off the twin satellites that orbited Mars.

Four signals then beeped steadily, clustered together where the four people had been buried alive.

If the weight of the rock had not crushed them, they had about three days to live. That was as long as their oxygen and water tubes would last.

Back at the dome, a rescue team was being assembled. At best, they would be ready in another hour. Which meant anything and everything I could do quickly with the robot might make a crucial difference in the survival rate of those four people trapped in the cave-in.

Most terrifying of all, one of the g.p.u. signals came from the space suit of my best friend, Rawling McTigre, director of the Mars Project.

CHAPTER 2

Fast as my robot body moved toward the site of the cave-in, back in the dome my body was totally motionless in the computer lab room.

As usual, I was on my back on a narrow medical bed in the computer laboratory. I wore a snug jumpsuit, in military navy blue. My head was propped on a large pillow so that the plug at the bottom of my neck didn't press on the bed. This plug had been spliced into my spine when I was barely more than a baby, so the thousands of microfibers of bioplastic material had grown and intertwined with my nerve endings as my own body had grown. Each microfiber had a core to transmit tiny impulses of electricity out through the plug into another plug linked into an antenna sewn into the jumpsuit. Across the room a receiver transmitted signals between the bodysuit antenna and the robot's computer drive. It worked just like the remote control of a television set, with two differences. Television remotes used infrared and were limited in distance. This receiver used X-ray waves and had a 100-mile range.

As for handling the robot body, it wasn't much different

than the sophisticated virtual-reality computer games that Earth kids had been able to play for decades.

In virtual reality, you put on a surround-sight helmet that gives you a three-dimensional view of a scene in a computer program. The helmet is wired so that when you turn your head, it directs the computer program to shift the scene as if you were there in real life. Sounds come in like real sounds. Because you're wearing a wired jacket and gloves, the arms and hands you see in your surround-sight picture move wherever you move your own arms and hands.

With me, the only difference is that the wiring reaches my brain directly through my spine. And I control a real robot, not one in virtual reality. From all my years of training in a computer simulation program, my mind knows all the muscle moves it takes to handle the virtual-reality controls. Handling the robot is no different, except instead of actually moving my muscles, I *imagine* I'm moving the muscles. My brain sends the proper nerve impulses to the robot, and it moves the way I made the robot move in the virtual-reality computer program.

The robot has heat sensors that detect infrared, so I can see in total darkness. The video lenses' telescoping is powerful enough that I can recognize a person's face from five miles away. But I can also zoom in close on something nearby and look at it as if I'm using a microscope.

I can amplify hearing and pick up sounds at higher and lower levels than human hearing. The titanium robot has fibers wired into it that let me feel dust falling on it, if I want to concentrate on that minute level. It also lets me speak, just as if I were using a microphone.

It can't smell or taste, however. But one of the fingers is wired to perform material testing. All I need are a couple of specks of the material, and this finger will heat up, burn the material, and analyze the contents.

It's strong too. The titanium hands can grip a steel bar and bend it.

And it's fast. Its wheels can move three times faster than any human can sprint.

As I neared the hills at the end of the valley, I hoped everything the robot could do would be enough.

But that hope ended when I saw the tons of dark red rubble that blocked the cave entrance.

CHAPTER 3

"Dad . . ."

I spoke into the robot's microphone, knowing my words would reach my father in the dome.

"Tyce?"

"I am here," I said, my words drawn out and tinny-sounding through the robot's sound system.

"And?" he asked.

Most of the slope of the rocky hill was dull red, with jumbles of rounded rocks resting where they had been undisturbed for centuries. Directly in front of me, a lopsided heap of rock, twice the height of a man, was a much brighter red. This was rock in a new position, unweathered by the dust storms that covered Mars every spring.

"It does not look good," I answered. "The entrance to the cave is totally blocked."

I couldn't help thinking, *Every minute that passes is one minute less for Rawling and the other three trapped inside.*

"What's your infrared tell you?"

The robot was capable of seeing on infrared wavelengths, which was a really weird way of looking at the world. It could show me temperatures of different objects, so I didn't need light waves.

I switched to infrared.

It was -50° Fahrenheit, and the side of the hills showed up in my vision as a deep, deep blue. The rubble of the collapsed cave was slightly less blue because some heat had been generated from the kinetic force of the cave-in.

Two incredibly bright pinpoints showed up halfway into the hill, with halos around the pinpoints that went from white to red to orange to blue the farther they were from the pinpoints of heat at the center. To me, it looked like candle flames I'd once seen when testing the infrared spectrum, with the air getting cooler the farther it was from the candle.

I described this to Dad. All I could think of was that the bright heat was the remnant of an explosion. *But this expedition hadn't taken explosives.*

"Doesn't make sense to me either," Dad said when I finished telling him about it. "What about the important indicator?"

I knew what he meant because we'd talked about it earlier.

The important indicator: 98.6° Fahrenheit. The temperature of a living human. This should show up as orange somewhere in the deep blue of the ice-cold rocks. If the space suits had been ripped by falling rocks, the orange would show up like bleeding air.

"Negative, Dad," I said. "Looks like the space suits are intact."

"Let's pray that's what it is."

Dad didn't say what I couldn't help but fear. Either the space suits were holding their body heat, or there was too much rock between them and me for any infrared to make it through. If it was the second option, we might never reach them.

"Tyce," Dad said, "can you quickly beam me some video? That will give the rescue team a good idea of the equipment they'll need. Then go climb the hill and try infrared from a different angle."

What I really wanted to do was panic. I wanted to roll forward to the edge of the pile of rock rubble and begin pulling rocks off as fast as I could. I wanted to shout for Rawling.

But I knew we'd all have to work together—and fast—for the scientists to survive. So I adjusted the robot's focus to allow its front video lens to survey the site.

I started with a wide angle, sweeping from the top of the hill. In the background there was a flash of the butterscotch Martian sky. My video picked up the rocks and the small shadows behind the rocks. I zoomed in closer on the cave-in site, confident the robot's computer drive was translating all of this in digital form and relaying the images back to the computer at the dome.

Just then Dad's voice came through loudly. "What's going on here?" he asked sternly. I'd never heard him so angry.

"I am sending you a video feed," I said, puzzled. "Is it not clear enough?"

"I demand an explanation for this!" he said, as if he hadn't bothered listening to my reply.

Why was he so upset? I was doing exactly what he'd asked.

"I'm sorry, Dad," I said. "I thought—"

"This is ridiculous," his voice blurted in my audio. "You can't walk in here with weapons and—"

There was a thud and a low groan.

My audio cut short.

Weapons? Had he been talking to someone in the computer lab? But weapons . . .

9

"Dad!" I shouted. "Dad!"

No answer.

What was happening back at the dome?

I pictured the computer lab. My body was on the bed, strapped in. I wore a blindfold and headset to keep any noise from distracting me. My wheelchair was beside the bed. If I shouted the mental command to take me away from the robot, I would return to consciousness there in total helplessness, unable to release myself from the straps, unable to see or hear a thing until someone released me. *If someone else instead of my dad was now in the lab, armed and willing to do damage . . .*

I was just lying there, with no way to protect myself. Yet this robot was too far away from the dome. It would take me 20 minutes to get it back and another 10 minutes to make it through the air locks at the dome entrance. Even if I made it back in time to protect my body with the robot, all they had to do in the lab was disconnect the computer, and the robot would be disabled.

And was I willing to take that long gamble and leave the cave-in with four people buried and in desperate need of help?

"Dad?" I tried again. I hoped all of this had been my imagination. "Dad? Dad?"

"Knock it off, kid," a strange voice replied.

"Who are you?" I asked. "Where's my dad?"

This was totally weird, like being in two places at once and helpless in both.

"What's happening there?" I shouted.

Without warning, it seemed like a bomb exploded in my brain. The red sand of the Martian valley fell away from me as instant and total blackness descended.

CHAPTER 4

I woke with a headache, as if someone had been pounding pieces of glass into my brain. While I was at the cave-in site, one of the goons must have simply clicked the "Off" switch to bring me back from the robot body.

This, too, had happened once before when I'd been suddenly disconnected from the robot computer. That other time, however, Rawling had been in the computer lab. He'd taken off my headset and blindfold before I woke.

Now, though, I was totally cut off from sight and sound. I felt the fabric of the bed against my fingers.

I nearly blurted out the first question that came to me. *Who is there?* I wanted to ask.

Where is my dad? I wanted to continue. *What have you done? Get me out of the straps and the blindfold and the headset.*

But I resisted all of what I wanted to say.

Helpless as I was, I only had two weapons.

The first was surprise. So I didn't move. I waited.

And waited.

And waited.

And while I waited, I used my most important weapon.

I prayed. With all the crises I'd been through lately on Mars—first an oxygen leak; then a tekkie attacked by unknown creatures; the opening of some strange black boxes; and, most recently, the discovery that my virtual-reality Hammerhead torpedo was real—I'd come to believe in God. And that he could be trusted, even when things looked really bad.

As they did for me, and for my dad.

The suspense in my total silence and darkness was horrible. Someone could be standing directly above me with the weapons I'd heard my dad mention. Someone could have that weapon pointed at me, finger on the trigger, about to squeeze. Or it could be a knife . . . or . . .

I waited, heartbeat by heartbeat, with my head throbbing in agony.

When it happened, I nearly jerked my body a couple of inches off the bed.

It was a hand. On my shoulder. Shaking me.

I managed not to flinch. I pretended I was a rag doll.

The hand shook me again and again and again.

I concentrated on staying relaxed. It wasn't easy. The shaking grew rougher and rougher, until it disconnected my neck-plug from the jumpsuit plug. My head hurt so bad from the sudden disconnection from the robot that I wanted to throw up.

When the shaking finally stopped, I felt the hands at my head. The headset was jerked from my ears.

"Stupid kid," I heard a voice mutter. I knew I'd heard that voice before, but I couldn't remember who it belonged to.

"You can't blame it on him, you idiot," another vaguely familiar voice said. "Jordan warned us there could be brain damage if you shut the program down without giving warning."

Jordan!

Dr. Jordan was the new scientist, just arrived from Earth. He'd designed the Hammerhead space torpedo that I'd refused to test because I believed it would be used as a weapon against Earth. (See Mission 4: *Hammerhead*.) Was Jordan behind this? But how could he be? He'd been locked up for five days, awaiting deportation back to Earth on the next shuttle.

"Well, if the kid's old man had just listened to us . . . ," the first voice grumbled.

"It seems you did plenty of damage to the kid. Jordan's going to be mad about that too."

What had they done to Dad? And who were they?

I clenched my teeth to keep from yelling.

Fingers plucked at my blindfold. I kept my eyes shut as the slight pressure of it left my cheek and forehead.

The hand shook me again. I played like the rag doll. I didn't know if it would help for them to think I was unconscious, but it seemed the best chance I had, no matter how small.

"Help me lift him into the wheelchair," voice one said. "He's out like a clubbed fish."

"I don't want to bring him to Jordan like this, though," voice two answered. "Then we'll have too much to explain."

"We might not have any choice. If the kid's brain circuits are scrambled, he'll never come out of this. Jordan's going to kill us for it."

"If Jordan's going to go nuts on us anyway, what will five minutes hurt?" voice two said.

I strained to place a face with the voice. It came to me.

One of the security force. I'd been with him on the platform buggy during the dome's oxygen crisis.

That familiar voice continued. "Give the kid a chance to wake up. What he doesn't know won't hurt him, and he won't be able to say anything about this to Jordan."

"Five minutes then," voice one said. "We wait any longer . . ."

"I know, I know. In the meantime, let's drag the kid's old man out of here."

Drag Dad out? What had they done to him?

I heard scuffling. I told myself there was nothing I could do from my wheelchair. I told myself the best thing I could do for Dad was wait for an opportunity to help somehow.

It didn't work. I had to open my eyes.

I peeked and saw the backsides of two large men, who were lifting Dad by his arms and shoulders. They dragged him toward the door, with Dad's feet trailing behind him.

It had been the operation to put the plug in my neck that caused damage to my spine. The freedom of being able to control an incredible robot body had cost me the freedom of being able to move the legs of my own body.

I'd learned a long time ago not to feel sorry for myself because of my wheelchair. I'd learned to stop wishing that I could walk like most everyone else. But in this moment, with every nerve telling me to get up and run after the two men and attack them for what they'd done to Dad, I hated my wheelchair all over again.

The door closed behind them.

That left me alone.

And totally, totally unsure of what was happening.

CHAPTER 5

Five minutes.

Fortunately, I didn't need more than 20 seconds, because it looked like faking unconsciousness had worked. All I needed to do was wait those 20 seconds, go to the door, throw it open, and yell for help.

The area of the Mars Dome was about four of the football fields that I've read about on Earth. The main dome covered mini-domes—small, dark, plastic huts where each scientist and tekkie lived in privacy from the others—and experimental labs and open areas where equipment was maintained. The dome was only two stories tall. The main level held the mini-domes and laboratories. One level up, a walkway about 10 feet wide circled the inside of the dome walls. Altogether, about 200 people lived beneath the dome.

I knew all it would take was one good, long yell for nearly all of the people to hear me. Probably 50 of them would come running. When they did, not only would I be safe, but they'd see the two goons who were dragging away my dad. Then we'd get to the bottom of this. Then I'd be able to work with the robot again on the rescue attempt at the cave-in site.

I counted to 20. Then, to be sure, I counted to 10.

Slowly I rolled forward and opened the door. In front of me were mini-domes, arranged neatly in lines. I looked down the corridors between them. I stared long and hard, trying to make sense of what I saw.

I shut the door again and rolled back to where I'd been.

Outside the computer lab, more members of the security force were herding dozens and dozens of protesting scientists and tekkies into groups in the main open area of the dome. Yelling would do me no good. Not when it looked like the security guards each carried neuron guns.

What was going on?

Neuron guns. For a project like the Mars Dome, it was necessary to have a police force as protection for everyone. But regular weapons were too dangerous. Not only could stray bullets do serious damage to equipment and the dome, but guns that fired bullets could be stolen and used by the wrong person.

Neuron guns solved both problems. They worked by firing electrical impulses that disabled nerves and neurons. No damage to skin or muscle or bone. Nor would they work for someone who stole one. The guns were linked by satellite beam to the dome's main computer. A security code had to be entered before the guns were operative. Each gun was programmed by fingerprint recognition to a specific member of the security force. Even after a neuron gun was operative, it wouldn't work in the hands of the wrong person.

Except now it looked like everyone in the security force was working together.

But how had they programmed the mainframe computer

to operate the guns? Only Rawling had the code, and he was under a cave-in.

I sighed. It wasn't going to do any good to roll out into the corridors and begin asking questions.

Worse, I only had a little over four minutes until the security goons returned for me.

I forced my mind away from questions and back to what I could do to help Dad and myself.

I wheeled a tight circle and surveyed the computer room.

On the bed the blindfold and headset lay where the goons had dropped them. Those wouldn't do me any good. On the computer table was a small tool set with tiny screwdrivers and some pliers that a tekkie had left the day before after doing some maintenance work.

I pushed the wheelchair over, grabbed the tool set, and stuffed it down the back of my jumpsuit.

There were a couple of pens beside a pad of paper. I ripped off some paper, folded it, and stuffed it up one sleeve. I slipped the pens up my other sleeve. I hoped some of these items would come in handy later.

Other than that, the room only held the computer drive, now shut off and disconnected from the remote that sent X-ray information to the robot out on the surface of the planet. I understood why my head hurt so badly. Rawling said it was very, very important that I be the one to take my mind away from the robot controls because the electrical impulses of my brain were so closely intertwined with the computer. One of the goons must have simply clicked the "Off" switch to bring me back from the computer body, which was like jamming an electric prong into the side of my head.

I kept staring at the computer, knowing there was something I'd be able to do if I was ever left alone for a while. . . .

I reached down and reconnected everything. I powered up the computer again and left it on, grateful that the humming of the hard drive couldn't be heard above the whoosh of the vents that circulated fresh air through the dome.

With the computer on again, all I needed was more time alone. That would give me the chance to reconnect my neck-plug, which was still loose from when the goon had shaken me so hard. Then, with the neck-plug of my jumpsuit sending information to the remote in this room, and with the remote sending digital information ahead to the robot body, I'd be reconnected to the robot. It was more difficult without the blindfold and headset to keep out distractions, but it was possible. And if I could control the robot body, I could get it back into the dome and let it do all the things I couldn't do from my wheelchair.

I spun the wheelchair back toward the door and positioned it where the security goons had left me. I slumped my head forward and closed my eyes.

And waited for their return.

CHAPTER 6

"Where is it?"

Dr. Jordan had taken a chair and turned it backward. He sat in it, facing me, barely a foot away. We were in Rawling's office, where the security men had delivered me only five minutes earlier.

I had faked unconsciousness there, too, as I listened to Dr. Jordan yell at them for powering down the computer program without being sure I had returned from the robot controls. But I still hadn't learned anything about the situation in the dome.

After he'd finished yelling, Dr. Jordan had pinched my nose shut and poured water in my mouth until I had no choice but to gag and fight for air.

When I'd blinked my eyes open, he smiled and said, "I knew you were faking it." Then he pulled up the chair and asked the question that made no sense to me.

"Where is what?" I asked in return. Cold water soaked the front of my jumpsuit, but I refused to let him know it made me uncomfortable.

Dr. Jordan nodded at the security guard. He brought over a handheld metal scanner, the type used to search for metal in rocks. The guard flicked it on, and the wand began beeping as he passed it over me.

The search was quick. They found the tool set, pens, and paper and took those. But the metal scanner results evidently weren't enough to satisfy Dr. Jordan.

"So," Dr. Jordan said, "it's not on you. Where is it?"

"Where is what?" I repeated.

"Project 3."

"Project 3?"

"Don't play games with me," he warned.

His face was round, like his gold-rimmed glasses, which always seemed to bounce light so that it looked like he had two perfect circular mirrors in front of his eyes. His goatee was round too, and his nose was turned up at the end, showing the dark of his nostrils as two more circles. From a distance, I'd always thought he looked harmless, like an absentminded clown. Just five days ago, when I'd refused to take the space torpedo on a test flight, however, I'd learned he was anything but harmless. And he'd sounded like a military general rather than the scientist I was led to believe he was. Now, with him looming in front of me, I realized how big he really was. At this angle, without light bouncing off his glasses, I saw into his cold eyes. And I shivered.

"I'm not playing games," I said. "Where is my dad? What's happening in the dome?"

As the security guards had pushed me through the dome, I'd kept my head down like I was unconscious. But I still heard enough commotion and worried voices to know that something terrible was happening.

"I want to know where you have it." Dr. Jordan leaned forward and put his hands on my shoulders. I smelled stale coffee on his breath. He squeezed his fingers into the muscles of my shoulders with such force I almost gasped. "I want to know what Ashley told you about it."

Ashley. His daughter. And my only friend close to my age. Hearing her name stabbed me with such pain I had to look away.

Everyone knew she'd died on our test mission when she flew Dr. Jordan's space torpedo directly into Phobos, one of the moons of Mars. I wore a silver earring of hers on a chain around my neck. The earring was a small cross. She'd given it to me as a friendship pledge when I'd had to travel far away from the dome to check out the strange black boxes. (See Mission #3: *Time Bomb*.)

But then she'd become more and more secretive about her past, sidestepping any questions I asked. And she'd betrayed me by not telling me she was like me—a kid who could control robots through virtual reality.

When she'd chosen to pilot the Hammerhead torpedo, I thought she'd betrayed me again. And I'd been angry. But then she'd crashed the torpedo into Phobos, sacrificing herself to save millions on Earth from dying.

After that, I'd had a hard time facing life. She was my friend, and I hadn't trusted her to do the right thing. I'd stayed in my room for two days, not wanting to talk to anyone.

"Talk to me." Dr. Jordan grabbed my chin and forced my eyes to look into his again. "You have no idea what kind of trouble you just bought yourself."

Obviously, he wasn't too upset about Ashley. How could he be so cold about her death? His coldness made me angry. And gave me strength.

"I'm not the one in trouble," I said, clenching my teeth. "You are."

He laughed harshly. "Me?"

"There are four men trapped by a cave-in, and you're keeping me from trying to help them." I drew a breath. "Something's happening out in the dome, and you're here instead of trying to fix it. So maybe you're part of that too. Which means if no one is trying to get out to the cave-in and you're to blame, you'll be responsible for those four scientists' lives."

Dr. Jordan's laughter died into a tight, nasty smile.

"That's right," he said, lifting a hand from my shoulder and gesturing around at the office. "I'd almost forgotten. Your friend, Rawling McTigre. He's out there, isn't he?"

As director, Rawling had taken this office over from the previous director, Blaine Steven, who was under arrest because of the oxygen crisis and was about to be shipped back to Earth on the next shuttle. Steven had made his office the biggest single room in the dome. And Rawling hadn't yet had time to make any changes. On the walls were framed paintings of Earth scenes like sunsets and mountains. The former director had spent a lot of the government's money to get those luxuries included in cargo. But even a director didn't get bookshelves and real books. Cargo was too expensive. If people wanted books, they read them on DVD-gigarom.

"Not only is *Rawling* out there," I said, getting angrier, "there are three others. If you don't let me get back out there . . ."

He twisted my arm. "*Nobody* tells me what to do. Not even the president of the World United. Understand? And you fall so far below that I could crush you like stepping on a grape." He let that small smile return. "Tell you what. If you don't give me what I want, I'll make sure those four stay so long under all that rock that they become mummies. And I can promise you, your parents will be next to die."

My anger dissolved in instant fear, and my voice cracked. "Tell me what it is you think I have. I can't give it to you unless I know what you are looking for."

Dr. Jordan studied my face. "I almost believe you," he answered. "Except you're the only person Ashley would have told. And you're the only person who could use it."

"What?" I asked with desperation. "Just tell me what you want."

Instead of answering, he stood suddenly. He walked around behind me, too quickly for me to turn in my wheel-chair and follow.

I felt him grab the back of my jumpsuit.

He twisted roughly and yanked hard. The fabric ripped.

When he stood in front of me again, I understood.

In his hand was the plug from my jumpsuit, the one that fit into my neck-plug, the one connected to the antenna sewn into the jumpsuit.

Dr. Jordan dropped the small plug and patch of fabric into my lap.

"There," he said. "Now you'll never be able to connect to it. If I don't get it back, at least you won't be able to control it. And if you can't use it, no one can."

It. Did he mean the robot body? Surely he knew it was at the cave-in site. If he wanted it, all he had to do was wait until I'd returned with it.

"Please," I said, "just tell me what it is you think I have and—"

"Lock him up," he ordered the security guards. "We'll give him the rest of the day to decide whether he wants to help. When he's hungry enough, he'll talk. If not, we'll see if some damage to his parents opens his mouth."

Dr. Jordan turned sharply and left the office. As the door opened and closed, I heard the commotion out in the dome.

What was going on?

One of the security guys took the handles of my wheel-chair and began to push.

I didn't know where they intended to lock me up.

All I knew was that the neck-plug had been ripped from my jumpsuit, and I no longer had any chance of reconnecting to the robot. Which meant I was a prisoner of my wheel-chair.

With time running out for Rawling and the other three trapped in the cave-in.

With my dad injured and taken somewhere else.

With Mom in danger if I didn't tell Dr. Jordan what he wanted.

With some sort of takeover happening in the dome.

And with the nearest help the distance from Earth to Mars—50 million miles away.

CHAPTER 7

My new prison was a storage room. Its floor size was twice as big as my wheelchair, and the ceiling hardly higher than I could have reached by standing on top of my wheelchair and jumping with my hands stretched tall.

But of course, I could not stand. Or jump.

Nor could I even roll my wheelchair. The security guys had removed the bolts from the wheels. If I turned and moved in any direction, the wheels would fall off.

The security guys had also shut off the light above me, leaving me in darkness.

I felt totally helpless. It was the worst mess I'd been in the entire time I'd lived on Mars. Although I knew God was with me, even in the dark, I felt totally alone. I wished God could talk with me, like Ashley did. But sometimes it seemed like I was talking to the ceiling.

I sat in the darkness for a couple of minutes, staring at the crack of light from under the door. My eyes began to adjust to the dimness.

Then I got an idea.

"Hey!" I suddenly shouted. "Help! Help!"

My voice echoed in the cramped storage room.

Two seconds later the door opened. I blinked against the light that outlined two security guards.

"Shut your mouth, kid," the first guard said. "You're not going anywhere. And no one will be able to help you."

I hadn't really expected help. I'd just wanted to find out how close the guards were, if there were any.

He'd answered my question.

Two of them sat just outside the door.

Why was it so important to keep two guards in front of me when I was so helpless to do anything?

※

I realized this small storage area was familiar.

I had stood in front of it barely a week ago.

I'd been here with a robot controlled by Ashley. I'd just learned that she, like I, had a spinal implant that allowed her to control a robot through the brain impulses that normally move a body's muscles.

You see, as part of the long-term plan to develop Mars, scientists hoped to use robots, controlled by humans, to explore the planet. Humans need oxygen and water and heat to survive on the surface. Robots don't. But robots can't think or feel like humans.

But what if technology made it possible for your brain to be wired directly into the controls of a robot? Then wouldn't you be able to see, hear, and do everything the robot could?

Well, that's me. Through a spinal transplant, I was the first human to be able to control a robot as if it were an extension of the brain.

But not the last.

Ashley had arrived on Mars equipped with the second-generation of human robotics, able to control an even more sophisticated robot. With the portable robot pack, which is a mini-transmitter, she didn't have to be strapped to a medical bed in a computer lab.

And the surgeon who had done her operation on Earth had learned from my operation. He didn't make any mistakes that put her in a wheelchair. So she had the best of both worlds. A human body that worked the way it should. And the ability to control robot bodies.

If she was alive.

This room had held the Hammerhead, a prototype space torpedo capable of destroying targets as large as a small moon. The Hammerhead had been designed to be handled the same way I handled the robot. Except instead of handling it with remote X-ray beams, a person needed to be hooked up inside it. I'd only flown it in virtual reality, learning to control its moves in a simulated combat program on a computer.

Ashley had actually flown it once. When she'd headed straight for Phobos, accelerating to thousands of miles per hour before crashing directly into the moon.

The night I'd been in front of this storage area, I'd stopped Ashley's robot from destroying the space torpedo because I hadn't known Dr. Jordan's true plans for it.

My heart twisted with sadness and regret as I thought about it.

If I'd allowed Ashley to wreck the Hammerhead then, she wouldn't have had to fly it. And if she hadn't had to fly it, it wouldn't have taken her into the surface of a moon at a speed fast enough to fuse the moon's rock into a gigantic crater.

But . . .

There was still some hope in my heart.

When I'd woken up yesterday, the fourth day after the crash, I'd been startled. On the seat of my wheelchair was an earring just like the one on a silver chain around my neck. As if someone had placed it there while I slept.

Only Ashley had the matching earring.

Or so I thought.

But in the time since, I hadn't seen her. I'd begun to wonder if the earring on my wheelchair was someone's idea of a very mean joke. When the cave-in had occurred, all my thoughts had turned to Rawling and the three others still trapped.

And then . . .

This.

All of this.

In the dimness, I stared at nothing and tried to block out all my fear and worry.

And I did the only thing I could do. I prayed again.

CHAPTER 8

"Why do I always have to deal with you?"

The door to the storage area had opened, and a large man filled the doorway. I couldn't see the features of his face because of the shadows behind it, but I definitely knew who it was. In the time I'd had to think in the dark, I'd realized that Dr. Jordan had to be working with someone who used to be high up at the Mars Dome. And because I trusted Rawling, that could be only one person.

Ex-director Blaine Steven.

During the oxygen crisis (Mission #1: *Oxygen Level Zero*), I'd disobeyed Steven's direct orders. He'd lost his directorship over mishandling the crisis. Then, later, when Dad and I and Rawling left the dome for a three-day expedition, Blaine Steven had once again taken over the Mars Dome (Mission #3: *Time Bomb*). Only our successful return had stopped him. But now it looked like, once again, he'd been released from his arrest. And that meant he and Dr. Jordan had to be working with some high-level people somewhere on Earth. It looked like those people wanted to use the Mars Project for their own means—to control the

Earth—instead of helping to accomplish the Project's original purpose.

Unlike with Dr. Jordan, I knew exactly what Steven meant by his question.

"Shouldn't you be worrying about how to deal with the cave-in instead?" I asked as an answer. "And what about everything else happening in the dome?"

He stepped forward. The two security guys stood behind him. He switched on a light in the storage room.

The room was so small and Steven so close that I could only see his jumpsuit where it stretched over his belly. I tilted my head back to look upward.

Mostly what I saw was chin and nose. His face seemed chipped out of a boulder, with thick, wavy gray hair and eyebrows to match.

He knelt down so we were at eye level, like he was a good guy trying to be helpful. But from past experience, I knew better.

"Listen," he said, "it's not good for Dr. Jordan to be this upset. Tell him what he wants, and everything else will go a lot easier."

"Everything else?"

Blaine Steven sighed. "You have a bad habit of asking questions when you should be giving answers."

He ran his hands through his hair and stood again. He stepped out of the storage room and returned with a chair. He sat on it and stared hard at me with his icy blue eyes. If he was trying to scare me, it didn't work.

"Everything else?" I repeated.

"Here it is in short," he said. "Everyone under the dome has been taken hostage."

"Hostage! But—"

"If you want me to explain, learn to listen."

I snapped my mouth shut.

"You probably won't be able to understand because you were born on Mars. You have no idea what it's like on Earth."

I had some idea. I knew our presence on Mars was a long-term plan—taking place over 100 years—to make the entire planet a place for humans to live outside the dome. I knew people on Earth desperately needed the room. Already the planet had too many people on it. If Mars could be made a new colony, then Earth could start shipping people here to live. If not, new wars might begin, and millions and millions of people would die from war or starvation or disease.

I didn't tell Blaine Steven this. He knew it already, and I was determined to listen until he finished.

"Although Earth has been at peace for 20 years because of the World United Federation," Steven continued, "a lot of political things have been happening beneath the surface of this calm. You don't pull together a federation of hundreds of countries and expect it to be perfect. In fact, with some of the bigger countries trying to take more water and resources from the smaller countries, the entire planet has been on the verge of war for the last 10 years."

I knew this. Rawling and I had spent time talking about it.

"Much of the prewar fighting has been done using a very ancient method. Spies."

My throat tightened. Rawling had talked about this too.

Blaine Steven smiled. "I'm proud to tell you," he said, "that I am one of them. I put my country far above the Federation and have secretly served my own government for 20 years, assisted often by contacts high in the military."

I couldn't help but interrupt. "Like Dr. Jordan."

His smile thinned. "Like Dr. Jordan."

"He's your boss," I said.

"He and I are working together for the same cause. And the time is right to take action. Taking 200 people hostage with only a handful of men is very simple when the only weapons on the planet are in your control."

"But why?"

"We have a number of people on Earth in prison for political crimes against the World United. Roughly 200. Once they are released, everyone here will be released. Rest assured, the media on Earth will give us so much coverage that the World United will have no choice but to give in."

"Four men are dying in a cave-in," I said. "Someone needs to save them."

"But that just adds to the drama," he answered with a sly smile. "As does the fact that the shuttle back to Earth has to leave in the next few days, or lose the only chance to make the right orbit for another six months."

My throat tightened again. Dad was the pilot. I knew very well how crucial the Mars-Earth-Mars shuttle was to our survival. The journey had to be carefully planned so that it occurred when Earth and Mars were nearest each other—roughly 50 million miles apart. At any other time, their orbits placed the planets up to double or triple the distance apart.

I protested. "If the shuttle doesn't leave, we'll run short of supplies."

"Exactly. Which just adds more pressure to the World United Federation." He laughed. "Of course, what they don't know is that a select group of the highest military men is planning a takeover anyway."

He tapped my shoulder. "And all of us can thank you for it."

"Me?"

"You. The guinea pig. We've been planning this since before you were born. Once you proved how successful the spinal implant could be, we went ahead and perfected the operation on others. You, and what you can do, make for a perfect military weapon. Space torpedoes and remote-controlled robots! Unstoppable."

I closed my eyes briefly. "Wrong," I said. "I have to choose to help. And I won't."

"Perhaps," he said, his voice silky. "Or perhaps not. Remember we're holding your parents hostage."

I could think of nothing to say to this.

"And there are, of course, the others."

Others. Ashley had had the operation. And the night I'd caught her trying to destroy the Hammerhead, she'd whispered, "There are others. Like us. And we are their only hope." So Ashley was right. But where were these others?

Blaine Steven frowned. I think at himself, not me. "Tyce, let me give you some advice. Tell Dr. Jordan what he wants."

"I probably would," I said, "but I don't know what he's looking for."

He exhaled. "You've always been stubborn. Even as a kid. You'd only been walking a few months when you had the operation that cut into your spinal nerves. After the surgery you spent hours and hours trying to get to your feet again. You refused to accept the fact that your legs wouldn't work for you. You never cried, just kept trying to push up. Again and again. I confess, I felt a lot of sympathy for you."

He shook his head in disgust. "Now? Your stubbornness makes me so angry that I'm glad the operation took your legs away from you."

He turned and stopped at the doorway. "Whenever you are ready to tell us what we need, just shout. Until then, enjoy your solitude."

The door closed, leaving me again in darkness. But this time it was a darkness of body and soul. What he didn't know was how much his words about my walking and the surgery had hurt.

CHAPTER 9

Some people twiddle their thumbs or tap their fingers when they're bored or nervous or impatient. Me? I juggle. And because I've done it so much, I don't even have to concentrate anymore. Especially with the gravity on Mars much lower than on Earth.

I always keep my three red juggling balls in a small pouch hanging from the armrest of my wheelchair. So in the darkness I took them out and began to juggle.

I hoped it would keep my mind away from all my fears.

It didn't.

My thoughts kept bouncing around, just like the balls I kept in the air in the darkness.

First, I thought about Rawling and how horrible it must be for him if he was even still alive—trapped, with tons of rock on top, not knowing if he would ever be rescued. I thought about what it would be like for the oxygen in his suit to slowly run out or for him to begin to die of thirst. When I got to that point, I desperately tried to think about something else.

Which led me to worrying about Mom and Dad and the hostage situation. I began to wonder what might happen if the political prisoners on Earth were not released. And I began to fear for all of us even more. But then I heard my mom's voice in my mind, and I knew what she would say. She was famous for sharing thoughts from the Bible in tough times, and the one that now leaped to my mind was: "Don't worry about anything; instead, pray about everything. Tell God what you need. . . . If you do this, you will experience God's peace." It was a verse she'd hammered into my head all my life, even before I'd believed in God. I used to roll my eyes at her. But right now remembering those words gave me the kind of peace I needed, especially when I felt so desperate.

I started to ask myself questions. Who were the "others" Blaine Steven had mentioned? Had Ashley been one of them? Where were they? And what did Dr. Jordan think I'd taken from him?

Then I remembered Blaine Steven saying he was glad the operation had taken away the use of my legs, and I began feeling sorry for myself. I wondered, for the umpteenth time, how my life would have been different without that operation.

After all, I'm the only person in the entire history of humankind who's only lived on Mars. Everyone else here came from Earth eight Martian years ago—15 Earth years—as part of the first expedition to set up a colony. The trip took eight months. During this voyage Kristy Wallace, a scientist, and Chase Sanders, a space pilot, fell in love. I was born half a Mars year after their marriage, which now makes me 14 Earth years old. The dome's leaders hadn't planned on any marriages or babies until the colony was better established, so they were shocked when my mom announced she was having me. Because my birth on the planet made dome life so complicated, my mom was forced to make a decision: either send me back to Earth or allow me to undergo an experimental surgery.

Mom knew that a baby couldn't take the G-force of inter-planetary travel and that a trip back to Earth would kill me. So she had no choice but to agree to the surgery. And dur-ing the surgery my spinal nerves had been cut, which meant I'd spend my life in a wheelchair.

But just as I was starting to feel the most sorry for myself, I remembered Rawling. At least I wasn't under tons of rock and dying slowly.

From there, my thoughts began a big circle all over again.

Finally I decided the best thing I could do was sleep.

I let the balls drop one by one and caught them, then put them away.

It was awkward and slow, but I pushed myself out of my wheelchair and curled up on the floor.

Somehow I managed to fall asleep.

CHAPTER 10

I don't know how much time passed until I woke. But when I did and yawned and stretched, something strange tickled my fingers.

My best guess was a slip of paper.

Which was very, very odd.

If someone had opened the door to put it there, I know I would have woken up. Besides, who would have been able to get past the two guards right out front?

The only two people who had already gotten past the guards were Dr. Jordan and Blaine Steven. I couldn't imagine them putting a slip of paper in my hand instead of waking me up and yelling at me again.

Not only was the *who* and the *how* strange, but so was the *why*.

The only reason I could think of for anyone to do this was to deliver a message. Of course, if there was a message, maybe then I'd get my answers to all three questions.

Unfortunately, reading in the dark is not a specialty of mine. I had learned to juggle a few years ago, I could handle robots and space torpedoes in virtual-reality and real-life situations, and I could whistle Christmas carols very badly, but I couldn't read in the dark.

I crawled forward and pushed my hand toward the crack of light that came under the door. Then I angled the slip of paper and squeezed my head as close to it as I could.

I couldn't even see my fingers clearly, let alone any handwriting on a piece of paper.

A solution, however, did occur to me. About the same time I also became aware of another, equally pressing need. I knew about an old Earth saying: "Kill two birds with one stone."

I crawled back to my wheelchair and pulled myself slowly up into sitting position.

I folded the piece of paper and tucked it down the front of my jumpsuit.

Then I took a deep breath and yelled, "Hey, out there! Can you open the door?"

Within seconds, the door did open.

"What is it, kid?" the first security guy asked. "Scared of the dark?"

The other security guy laughed.

"Please," I answered them both, "can you put the bolts back on my wheels? I . . . um . . . need to go to the bathroom."

※

I guessed I'd been held prisoner in the storage room for less than a couple of hours. Still, it felt so good to be out under the dome that I already dreaded being put back into the darkness.

As the security guy pushed me away from the equipment area and past the laboratories toward the mini-dome living area, I looked around. Up, sideways, forwards.

The dome was strangely hushed.

Usually scientists and tekkies would be walking around in twos or threes, discussing their work or trading gossip. Usually, above me, on the second-story platform that ringed the inside of the dome, somebody would be jogging. And most always, there would be at least one person on the higher telescope platform.

Now, nothing.

"Where is everybody?" I asked, shifting in my wheelchair and trying to see past the legs of the guy pushing me.

He put a big hand on my head and twisted it so I was looking straight ahead again.

"No questions," he said. "Eyes forward."

Fear caused an icy lump in my throat. Why did the dome seem so empty?

My voice croaked out a question. "Was everybody marched out of the dome?"

I pictured what it would be like for 200 scientists and tekkies to be forced outside of the dome without space suits. The dome above protected us from a thin, frigid atmosphere of no oxygen and temperatures as low as -200° Fahrenheit. People would crumple in seconds and die in minutes. And what if Mom and Dad had . . .

"Relax, kid," the security guy said. "Jordan and Steven aren't that stupid. If they killed everybody here, they'd have nothing left to bargain with against the World United."

That made me feel a little better. But not much. Not if the only reason Jordan and Steven let people live was as bargaining tools. What if the bargain didn't work? Would they start killing people then?

We passed through the open space where people usually sat and relaxed in front of fake trees and a little park.

Just beyond were the mini-domes, clustered neatly in the living area of the main dome.

"Were you in on this from the beginning?" I asked, still looking straight ahead. "And when exactly was the beginning? Did Blaine Steven know from the first day he arrived on Mars that he might do this? Did you work for him from the first day? And—"

"You don't listen, do you? I said, no questions."

"Four people are trapped in a cave-in. My dad is hurt. I don't know where my mom is. I need to ask questions. So do you. Like, why aren't you helping?"

"Enough." He said it so angrily that I winced, waiting for him to hit the back of my head.

He didn't.

Instead, he turned the wheelchair sharply into the first mini-dome of the living area.

Except for some decorations and photos from Earth, this mini-dome was no different than the one I lived in with Mom and Dad. It had two office-bedrooms with a common living space in the middle. In ours, we didn't use the second room as an office, because that had become my bedroom. Another door at the back of the living space led to a small bathroom. It wasn't much. From what I've read about Earth homes, our mini-dome had less space in it than the size of two average bedrooms.

"This is the closest bathroom," he growled as he stopped in front of the door. "And be grateful I'm taking you here."

That told me plenty, that the takeover of the dome was so complete it didn't matter whose mini-dome we entered.

"It won't work," I said. "It's not big enough."

"Huh?"

"The only bathroom I can use in the dome is my own. It was made bigger to fit my wheelchair."

Without a word, he turned my wheelchair and pushed it back out of the mini-dome. It wasn't difficult to tell he was grumpy about all of this.

Thirty seconds later we reached our mini-dome. I tried to block out my sadness and fear that it was so empty without Mom or Dad around. I had a plan and needed to follow it, no matter how little chance it would give Rawling and the others. Time was running out.

"You can close the door, but leave it unlocked," the guard growled, stopping in front of our bathroom. "You've got one minute. Anything longer, and I come busting in to make sure you're not trying anything."

"Anything like what?" I asked. "Like running away and leaving my wheelchair behind?"

"One minute," he said. "Those are my orders."

"It's not enough," I said.

"Make it enough."

"You try living in a wheelchair," I said. "You'll find out why it isn't enough."

He sighed. "Just go. If that's what it takes to make you quiet. Go, go, go."

"One other thing," I said.

"What!"

I pointed at a box in the corner of the dome. It held Flip and Flop, the koala-like animals that Ashley and I had rescued. As usual, they were asleep.

"Can you change their water?" I asked the guard. "When they wake up, they like fresh water in their dish."

"Only if it gets you in and out of here as fast as possible."

I smiled at him. Sweetly.

He didn't smile back.

❋

I wheeled inside. The door shut. I rolled the wheelchair backward so that the handles touched the door. I set the brake on my wheelchair. If he tried opening the door, at least I had it blocked.

Although the bathroom was bigger than all the others in the dome, it still didn't have much room. Limited resources made it necessary that all space be used as efficiently as possible. There was a shower with a sitting bench, a sink with a cabinet beneath, and, most importantly, a toilet.

Much as I wanted to take the security guy's advice and go, go, go, I reached to the cabinet. It had shelves for tooth-paste, shaving cream, and stuff like that. Beneath the shelves a few towels were stacked neatly.

I reached for the shelf and quickly grabbed a few sleep-ing pills, hoping I'd have the chance to use them on the guards. Mom sometimes had migraine headaches and used them when she really needed to get to sleep. I leaned forward and slipped the pills into the top of my socks.

Then I took out the slip of paper.

I unrolled it. I'd been right. It was a note.

But I never would have guessed the message.

> Tyce. The only place I could think of is your bath-room. Look under the towels. Midnight tonight. Don't go anywhere. Just wait.

The note wasn't signed. At least not with a name.

The person who'd written it had drawn a tiny cross at the end of the message.

A cross like the one on the chain around my neck.

Ashley?

CHAPTER 11

Not enough time passed before the storage room door opened again. It made me glad I had decided to wait until later in the night to use what I'd found in the bathroom.

There had been a robot pack under the towels. Like the one Ashley had used to control her robot. Dr. Jordan had ripped the plug out of my jumpsuit, but I didn't need that anymore! Now I just needed to find time to control the robot body, and maybe I could help the hostages.

"Take him," Dr. Jordan said, standing outside. Light bounced from his glasses, so I couldn't see his eyes. The rest of his expression was unreadable.

Take me? Where? Did he somehow know what I'd found under the towels in the bathroom of my mini-dome?

I tried to keep my own face unreadable as the security guy stepped into the storage room and behind my wheelchair.

I made sure I leaned back in the wheelchair, as if I was so tired I didn't care.

But that wasn't true. I did care very much. And for the first time all day, I had something to hope for.

The security guy pushed me down the corridor outside the storage room.

The dome above was as dark as the Martian night. On most evenings by this time, I would have gone up to the telescope. Until I'd found freedom away from the wheelchair by controlling the robot, the best illusion of freedom I found was gazing into the outer reaches of the solar system and beyond.

"About seven hours have passed," I said to Dr. Jordan's back as the security guy pushed me. "It's not too late to help those people in the cave-in." I had to keep trying. Rawling would, if he were in my place.

Dr. Jordan didn't reply. He merely walked at a fast pace.

I could have kept up myself, just using my arms and pushing my wheels. But if I leaned forward at all, the security guy would have been able to see my lower back and what I had hidden there. So I remained sagged backward against the wheelchair and let them take me.

Soon enough I found out where we were headed.

To the dome entrance.

Where Mom and Dad stood, all alone, trapped in the air lock between the outer and inner doors of the dome.

❈

"It's simple," Dr. Jordan told me, hands behind his back as he stared through the clear, hard, plastic window into the air-lock chamber. "Tell me what I want, and I open the inner door. If not, I open the outer door. . . ."

I fully understood Dr. Jordan's threat.

The air lock stuck out of the dome, like the tunnels that stuck out of igloos in photographs I'd seen of Earth's far north. The outer door at the end of the tunnel led directly to the surface of Mars. The inner door of the air lock was right in front of us. If someone wanted to go outside, they first opened the inner door and stepped into the air lock in a space suit. With the outer door closed, no oxygen was lost when the inner door opened. Once the inner door was closed, the outer door could be opened. The small amount of air inside the air lock would disappear, turning instantly into a puff of white vapor as the warm, moist oxygen-filled air made contact with the Martian atmosphere.

But neither Mom nor Dad wore space suits. The only thing keeping them from the brutal cold and lack of oxygen was the outer door. Once it opened, they would live only as long as they could hold their breath.

"You should know from your Hammerhead experience," Dr. Jordan said, "that I'm not bluffing."

As he spoke, Mom and Dad walked toward the clear plastic window where I sat on this side.

Tears blurred my vision of them. Mom, with her short brown hair and concerned smile. Dad, with his square face and dark blond hair.

Mom pressed her fingers hard against the window as if she wanted to touch me. Dad stood beside her, arm around her shoulder. They were both shivering. A large bruise darkened the side of Dad's face.

I reached toward them, pressing the window with my fingers where Mom's hand was.

"Give me what I want!" Dr. Jordan ordered me. "Or you can watch them die."

I didn't remove my eyes from Mom and Dad.

"Do they know why you have them in there?" I asked.

"Of course. I gave them a chance first to tell me where you had it hidden. And they were as stubborn as you."

"It's because I don't know what you want. Neither do they." I wiped away a tear and tried to keep my voice from trembling. "Please don't do this."

Dr. Jordan answered by reaching past me to put his hand on the button for the outer air-lock door.

Mom and Dad saw his action. Dad took his hand off Mom's shoulder and put his index finger of one hand across the index finger of his other hand to make the shape of a cross. I knew he was reminding me of all the things we'd talked about whenever I asked him questions about God. Like the conversation we'd had after Ashley died. When he'd told me that there are some things we'll never understand until we can go to heaven and ask God face-to-face. That the important thing was to trust in God.

Dad put his arm around Mom's shoulder again and held her tighter.

"I want your answer in five seconds," Dr. Jordan said. He waited a beat and spoke a single word. "Five."

Mom lifted a hand and pointed at her eye. Then she touched the left side of her chest. Then she pointed at me. Eye. Heart. Me.

"Four," Dr. Jordan said calmly.

I love you. That's what her sign language meant. I love you.

"Three."

I quickly touched my eye and my chest above my heart and pointed back at them.

"Two."

"Please don't do this," I said. "Please."

"One."

I grabbed at his hand, but it was like trying to pull away a bar of iron.

He hit the button.

At the far end of the air lock, the door slid open.

And a white puff of vapor took away all the air that Mom and Dad could breathe.

CHAPTER 12

Dad pulled Mom in toward him, as if he could shield her from the vicious cold vacuum of the Martian atmosphere. He buried his face in her hair.

They were so close that if I could have put my hand through the window, I would have been able to touch both of them. Yet I was helpless to do anything but watch.

I tried to keep my voice as calm as possible.

"There is nothing I can tell you," I said to Dr. Jordan. "If there was, I would tell you now."

"I think you are lying to me."

"Put me in the air lock instead of them. It's not their fault I don't know what you want."

Dr. Jordan studied my face. I lifted my eyes briefly to his, then watched Mom and Dad again. He clutched her, and her arms held him just as tight. How much longer could they hold their breath? I wondered if it would help to tell Dr. Jordan about the note and tonight's meeting. But that wasn't what he wanted. Still . . .

"What do you want?" I pleaded. "At least give me the chance to answer you."

I was ready to throw away the only hope I saw for any of this. The robot pack I'd found under the towels.

Mom and Dad fell to their knees.

Dr. Jordan continued to study my face.

"Fine then," he said.

He hit the button to close the outer door lock. Seconds later, when it was shut, he opened the inner door lock. Oxygen-filled air from the inside of the dome whooshed into the air lock.

"Mom!" I shouted. "Dad!"

"Tyce!" Dad croaked.

Dr. Jordan pushed my wheelchair away from the window as Mom and Dad struggled to their feet.

"Bring them back in," he told the security guy. "I don't want to waste any hostages. If they die, it will be on video, so that all of Earth can see what happens if they don't do as we demand."

Dr. Jordan began to wheel me away.

I twisted frantically, trying to look back.

"Are you all right?" I heard Dad yell.

"Yes!" I shouted.

"Silence," Dr. Jordan said. "Or I'll put them back in there."

I bit my lower lip to keep from crying. They'd nearly died, yet Dad was concerned about how *I* was doing. It was that kind of sacrificial love that Mom and Dad had for me that had first convinced me there must be a God—and that he did care about me.

Seconds later, we were in the corridor leading back to the storage room. When we reached the storage room that was my prison, the other security guy stood from his chair in front.

Dr. Jordan shook his head and smiled sadly for my benefit. "I could almost admire your stubbornness," he said. "It's a pity you aren't one of ours."

One of ours? What did that mean?

Then Dr. Jordan's smile vanished as abruptly as the air had been sucked out of the air lock. "I'm wondering if you outbluffed me," he said. "So tomorrow I'm going to put them in the air lock again. But this time I promise I won't let them out alive unless I get what I want from you."

Back came the smile.

"Let him out once for a bathroom break," Dr. Jordan said to the security guy. "Just once. That's it until morning. He can brood in the darkness about how his silence is going to kill his parents."

CHAPTER 13

Hours later I was thirsty.

They had left water with me, but I hadn't touched any of it. With a meeting at midnight, I didn't want to risk the possibility of filling my bladder.

Those hours of thirst gave me plenty of time to think and wonder in my wheelchair in the silent, dark isolation of the storage room.

Was Ashley somehow alive? Or was someone setting me up? And if it was someone else, why?

One part of me desperately wanted to believe it was Ashley. I'd found the silver cross on my wheelchair, and only she could have left it there, right? Yet I'd seen her fly the Hammerhead into a moon. I'd seen the explosion, and later, I'd seen the crater the dome had named "Ashley's Crater" through the dome telescope. And if Ashley was alive, why was she in hiding? And why hadn't she secretly found a way to talk to me in the days since the explosion? Maybe someone else had stolen the silver cross from her before she died, and that someone just wanted me to believe Ashley was somewhere under the dome. But if that was the case, why?

All my hope hung on one single thing. The note. It had been signed with the shape of the cross of Ashley's earring. As if she had really placed it in my hand while I was sleeping. But that would have been impossible. The security guards would have seen her go into the storage room. I would have woken up as the door was opened. So I couldn't believe it was Ashley.

If not Ashley, then, who?

It seemed that only Dr. Jordan or Blaine Steven had the authority to direct the security guards. But how could Jordan or Steven have done it without waking me up? Why would either one give me the note? And the robot pack? Was one betraying the other by giving me the robot pack? Or was it just another way to try to get me to tell them what I didn't know?

And what was it that Dr. Jordan wanted so badly?

Whatever was happening, I had a lot more to worry about than just myself.

Rawling and the other three scientists were hours closer to running out of air. Mom and Dad were among the hostages and would face the air lock again tomorrow if I didn't give Jordan what he wanted. Two hundred hostages were being used as a bargaining tool in Dr. Jordan's game of war. We were less than two days away from the shuttle launch that was necessary to supply the dome.

Far more important than all of our lives, however, was that the Mars Dome had to survive—for the future of millions and millions of people on Earth. Phase 1 had been to establish the dome, and we were now in Phase 2: growing plants outside the dome so that more oxygen could be added to the atmosphere. Eventually people would be able to live on Mars.

That was long-term.

Now it seemed the short term was equally crucial. I knew enough about Earth politics to understand how easily wars started. World War I had begun because one person in a small European country was assassinated. Given the unrest of that time, it had been like a spark set among dry grass, and fighting had spread across Europe from there, dragging in the United States too. Now, with some of the World United countries ready to rebel, a hostage-taking on Mars might be all it took to start another world war. How many would die then?

I was too miserable in all my thoughts to even bother juggling.

I did what I often did in my quiet time.

I prayed.

Through the events of the last three months, I had come to believe in God. It sure helped. Not that I expected God to come in and automatically fix things for me whenever something went wrong. I'd learned there's evil and suffering all around us because of the choices people make. But having faith in God means you decide to trust him, even when you can't see the outcome. Since scientists are used to seeing results and proof, and since it's scientifically impossible to prove God exists, some of them want to think that the only things that exist are the things you can measure. Other scientists, though—like Mom and Dad and Rawling—think that a creator like God must be behind the amazing things of this universe, and they are able to take that last leap of faith to trust in him. You have to accept that he is in control.

Faith and trust, though, are much easier to lean on when things are good. During bad times, it's easy to wonder if God's really there and if he really cares. That's why prayer is even more important—because it helps you connect with God.

Mom once told me that it's easier to hear God in quiet times. A nudge in your heart, maybe, or new thoughts that help you deal with your problem.

It was easy to be silent in the storage room.

I prayed, asking God to help. But more importantly, I asked him to help me be as strong as possible, no matter what happened.

Then from the silent darkness around me came a tiny voice, floating near my head. "Tyce," it said from thin air, "listen to me without speaking!"

CHAPTER 14

My head and neck froze, but my eyeballs went side to side and up and down.

"God?" I whispered. "Is that you?"

After all, I *had* been praying to God. But somehow I hadn't expected him to answer. Why would God want to talk to me—out of all the people in the universe? On the other hand, maybe the voice was just my imagination. Was I going crazy, locked up in this dark room?

"Quiet!" the tiny, floating voice said quickly. "Don't bring the security guards in here!"

It has to be God, I thought, with a quick intake of breath. "But you could stop them so easily that—"

"Quiet, Tyce! Listen! I don't have much time!"

"OK," I whispered, feeling weird talking to God like this. *Had* I lost my mind?

A much louder voice interrupted. From outside the door. One of the security guys. "Kid, what do you want?"

"Huh?" I asked.

The door opened. It was night, and most of the dome lights had been dimmed. The guard stepped halfway into the storage room, which meant he almost filled it.

"What do you want? Is it time for your bathroom break?"

"No," I answered.

"What's going on then?"

"Just talking to myself."

Was I just talking to myself? Had I imagined the voice?

"Well, knock it off," the guard grunted.

"Sure," I said.

He slammed the door shut.

The silence returned to the darkness. I waited and waited, wondering if I would hear the voice again.

It came. Floating in the air.

"See?" the tiny voice said. "Told you not to make any noise. Are you ready to listen?"

If it was God speaking, he didn't have to point out that he was always right. But I wasn't going to say it. Not if it would bring the guard back and prove God right again.

"Tyce, take out the robot pack. Set it on the floor."

If I do that and the guard walks in . . .

"Tyce, take out the robot pack. Set it on the floor."

I *was* losing my mind.

"There is hardly any time left. Do it!"

Slowly I leaned forward. The robot pack had been digging into my lower back for so long I was grateful to pull it loose. I hesitated, then finally leaned over and set it on the floor.

This is crazy. Really. If the guard walks in and finds it . . .

I waited for the voice to say something else. It didn't. I couldn't risk speaking again, so I couldn't even ask what was happening.

"Finished," the tiny, quiet voice said a few minutes later. "You can take the robot pack again. Don't wait until midnight. Plans have changed. Instead, count to 2,000, then get into the robot body. And don't panic. Remember that. Don't panic at what you see."

Panic?

"But—"

"Shhh. I'm gone."

I waited for more.

Nothing came.

I began to count.

I stopped counting briefly and did some math. Sixty seconds in a minute. So 2,000 seconds was roughly . . . half an hour.

That's all I needed to wait to find freedom beyond the wheelchair and this dark, cramped storage room.

⚛

Finally I finished counting and leaned forward in my wheelchair. With difficulty, I reached behind me and fumbled with the connections until the robot mini-transmitter was securely attached to my neck-plug.

I hoped Ashley was the one who'd left the note and the robot mini-transmitter for me. I hoped she'd be near the robot when I took control of it.

But along with all my other worries, I now had one more.

What was there not to panic about when I finally got into the robot body?

CHAPTER 15

Normally, I'd be in the computer lab for any robot control activation. Rawling would insist on a checklist. He'd tell me it was just like flying, that preparation and safety had to be first.

He'd strap my body to the bed so I wouldn't accidentally move and break the connection. He'd warn me against any robot contact with electrical sources. He'd remind me to disengage instantly at the first warning of any damage to the robot's computer drive since harm to the computer circuits could spill over to harm my brain. And then he'd blindfold me, strap my head in position, and soundproof me.

This was different. I'd never used the mini-transmitter that Ashley did. Good thing it didn't need to connect through the antenna sewn into my jumpsuit. Dr. Jordan, of course, had ripped out that plug.

I assumed this mini-transmitter was programmed to her robot, and the controls would be similar to mine.

I assumed, too, she—or whoever had left the note and mini-transmitter—was waiting near the robot to meet me as soon as I began to control the robot body.

In other words, very, very soon I'd find out who'd left the note and mini-transmitter for me.

I closed my eyes and leaned back. I hit the power button and waited for the familiar sensation of entering the robot computer.

In the darkness and silence and intensity of my concentration, it came.

I began to fall off a high, invisible cliff into a deep, invisible hole.

I kept falling and falling and falling. . . .

⚛

I'd expected to see the walls of mini-domes, the floors, the roof of the dome. I'd expected to see a person—hopefully Ashley.

Instead, the images sent to my brain were unreal and bizarre.

Two large dark caves filled my whole vision. Below those caves were two horizontal rows of huge, shiny, white, rectangular rocks. They seemed to be stuck into the face of a weird, smooth mountain.

What scared me the most was that the mountain began to move!

And when the mountain moved, it roared! A hot wind rushed ahead with the roar!

I remembered the warning given to me by the tiny, floating voice. *"Don't panic."*

That warning was the only thing that kept me from screaming in fear.

I watched the mountain move more and told myself that none of this was actually happening to me in the wheelchair, but to a robot body. I told myself the robot body digitally translated the sound waves and the sensation of heat and the pressure of the wind, which my brain retranslated as actual events. I was safe, even if the robot body was not.

It helped.

But only a little.

Suddenly the ground beneath shifted and thrust me upward!

Two gleaming balls, white with dark centers, filled my vision.

I couldn't help it. I spun and turned and fled.

Right off the edge of a cliff.

I screamed as I fell. My vision became a swirling blur. I knew I had to disconnect before the robot body smashed to pieces and destroyed the computer drive.

But I didn't have time.

Just as suddenly the ground appeared beneath me again. I bounced but stayed upright. Before I could relax, the ground moved horizontally, carrying me away from the roaring windy mountain of twin black caves and shiny rocks and monstrous gleaming balls.

When the ground stopped moving, I looked around.

The ground was pale, with grooves leading in all directions.

A dark, long bridge stretched upward toward the mountain of caves and shiny rocks and gleaming balls. Each side of the mountain was covered with long, black fabric.

Except now I was far enough away from that mountain to make sense of it.

It wasn't a mountain.

It was a face.

The dark caves were nostrils. The two horizontal rows of shiny rocks were teeth. The monstrous gleaming balls were eyes. The black fabric hanging on each side of the mountain was hair.

That meant . . .

I looked at the ground beneath me and the long bridge stretching up toward the face.

That meant I was sitting on a hand. And the long bridge was an arm. I had run the robot body off the hand, and the hand had caught me and shifted me back away from the face.

Impossible!

I stared for several more seconds, and the face began to make more sense to me. I knew that face.

My voice squeaked, high and tiny, as I spoke a single word.

"Ashley?"

CHAPTER 16

Ashley. Not dead, but alive.

Very alive.

I stared at her like I was seeing her for the first time. Of course, with her looking so huge to me, it kind of *was* seeing her for the first time.

To say I was glad to see her is the understatement of the year!

"Ashley," I said again, still in shock. To me, my voice sounded like it did during the terrible months when it broke into a high pitch when I least expected it. "You *weren't* in the Hammerhead! How did you get out?"

She opened her mouth. Again I was hit with a loud roar.

This time, however, I knew what it was. Ashley's voice. I made an adjustment, and the roar dropped in volume.

". . . tell you about that later," she said in a whisper. "We don't have much time. With all the hostages together in one spot, they are using infrared detectors to search the dome."

Infrared detectors. Looking for body heat. With 200 people wandering around the dome, it would have been impossible to spot her. But now . . .

"Move to the power plant," I squeaked. "It throws so much heat you'll never be seen against the backdrop."

"Tyce," she said patiently, "I *am* hidden near the power plant."

I looked around, trying to make sense of my surroundings. But I couldn't. Sitting on the palm of Ashley's hand, everything was so gigantic to me that it was totally distorted.

I took a moment to appreciate what it meant to control a robot this tiny. I looked down at the robot's legs and arms and hands. All of it looked identical to a full-sized robot. I wiggled its fingers, spun a quick circle. It worked the same too. The only difference was its size.

"Wow," I said to Ashley.

"Wow?"

"This is a great robot!"

"Should be," she said with a tight smile. "It only cost about $15 billion to develop. You're the size of an ant right now. In fact, that's what it's called. An ant-bot."

I had plenty of questions for her. How did she know about the development costs? How had she gotten control of the ant-bot? How did she know they were using infrared to search for her? Most of all, how had she survived the crash of the Hammerhead space torpedo? And how had she arrived back on Mars?

"Look," she said. "On Earth, the scientists see unlimited use for people like you and me. Once we've learned the controls of a robot, we can handle just about any machine designed on the same principles. Aircraft, submarines, space torpedoes, ant-bots. Basically, it's like being able to use human brains to control equipment by remote control."

"An ant-bot, though. What good is that?"

"Are you kidding?" she said. "Medical procedures.

Think of how easily an ant-bot could do small-scale surgery. Computer repair. Anything that's too delicate for human fingers, the ant-bot does no problem." She frowned. "But that's not why Dr. Jordan wanted it designed. He's just interested in robots as weapons."

Yes. The Hammerhead space torpedo.

Her tomboyish grin finally appeared. "What's great is that I've been using it against him. I've been able to do a lot of spying. That's how I know he thinks I'm still alive and is going to search with infrared. That's how I was able to get past the security guys who were guarding you in front of the storage room."

It was very weird, sitting on the palm of her hand and listening to her speak.

"At first, Tyce, when I used the ant-bot to get you the note, I thought it would be better to let you get into my big robot. But this afternoon Dr. Jordan locked it away. You wouldn't have been able to get out. So I risked talking to you and reprogrammed your mini-transmitter to activate this robot. I needed to be able to speak to you, and I couldn't while you were being held prisoner."

In that minute I decided I was never going to tell her I'd thought she was the voice of God. I could figure it out now, at least. She'd hidden herself near the dome's power plant, then used her own mini-transmitter to control the ant-bot. She'd raced in the ant-bot to the storage room where I was hidden and told me to set the mini-transmitter on the floor. Then she'd done the reprogramming so that I'd wake up in the ant-bot instead of the regular robot. That's when she gave me the new instructions to wait 2,000 seconds—the half hour it took her to get the ant-bot back here to the power plant. Once the ant-bot was close to her again, she'd ended the control, lifted the ant-bot onto her palm, and waited for *me* to begin controlling it.

"I'm impressed," I said, "that you knew where to hide the mini-transmitter for me."

"You're my best friend," she said. "How many times before had I waited for you to go all the way across the dome instead of using the nearest bathroom? It was easy for me to guess that you'd eventually get there."

My ant-bot face was not capable of smiling, but inside, I had the world's biggest smile. *Best friend. I like the sound of that.*

"So if we don't have much time," I said, "what are we going to do?"

"I've done my count," she said. "Altogether, there's only six security guards. That's all they need, because the guards have weapons and the scientists and tekkies don't. If we can get both our robots working together, we might have a chance to fight the guards."

"Robots working together?" I said. "How? Your robot is locked up."

"Easy," she said. "Get your robot to unlock it."

"My robot is 10 miles away." I paused for a second, thinking of the cave-in. It looked like the only hope of rescue was in first stopping Dr. Jordan and Blaine Steven. "I can get it here in 20 minutes, but I'll still need to get it inside the dome. Someone would notice for sure."

She nodded. "I've thought of that. If we can get the hostages to create a distraction, we'll use it to bring your robot through the air lock."

"Big if . . . ," I said. I was finally getting used to my squeaky voice. "All of the hostages have got to know exactly when to start a distraction. How do you do that?"

"The hostages are all gathered in the meeting room.

Easier to guard them that way. We sneak the ant-bot in and tell one or two. They'll tell the rest."

Although it was a great idea, I nearly laughed. When the ant-bot crawled onto their shoulders, how many of *them* would think the voice of God was whispering in their ears?

"So," I said, "you and I just need to figure out the timing on all of this."

"Yes," she said. "And soon. Dr. Jordan has sent a message to the World United. If the prisoners on Earth aren't freed within another hour, Dr. Jordan is going to execute a scientist here under the dome. He's going to send live video coverage of the execution by the satellite feed, so that the media will get it and broadcast it all across Earth."

"What!"

"And Dr. Jordan says he'll execute someone else every half hour after that until the Earth prisoners are freed. He believes public pressure will make the Federation do what he wants."

"Tell me," I said. "Please tell me Dr. Jordan is not your father."

Ashley took a deep breath. "No. And that's a whole other story. There's 24 of us, not including you."

"Twenty-four. On Mars?"

"No. I was the one they picked to send here. I was supposed to help Dr. Jordan. Because they didn't think you'd help once you knew what they wanted."

"They?"

"I don't have enough time to tell you everything right now. Dr. Jordan is not a scientist. He's high up in the military and part of a secret group of men with power and money and military control. They're the ones who set up all the experiments on the 24 of us. They want to overthrow the World United and—"

She stopped.

Without warning, my world turned black and swirled and shifted again.

It took me a second to figure it out. She had closed her hand around the ant-bot, then moved her hand quickly.

But why?

An instant later, from the darkness inside her closed hand, I understood.

"Dr. Jordan!" she said. "How did you—"

"You foolish, foolish girl!" Dr. Jordan's voice hissed. "I'm going to make you pay for all the grief you've caused me."

CHAPTER 17

I pushed ahead, bumping into the solidness of her fingers. A crack of light gave me guidance, because she wasn't pressing her hand together very hard. I buzzed toward that crack of light.

"I knew we'd find you eventually," Dr. Jordan said. "The dome isn't big enough for you to hide forever."

There wasn't enough room to squeeze through her fingers. I reached out and jabbed as hard as I could. Her fingers opened slightly, and I burst through. Her hand was cupped, and I was able to make progress up the inside of her wrist.

"It's not right what you're doing to the scientists and tekkies." This was Ashley's voice. "Your fight is on Earth, not here."

The fabric of Ashley's jumpsuit loomed in front of me like an ocean of blue. I grabbed it and pushed up, then slid underneath, letting the fabric of her sleeve drop.

"My fight is anywhere it takes to win." Hidden as I was, his voice still reached me clearly. "You of all people should know that."

"I don't believe in your fight anymore."

"Obviously," he answered. "But the rest do. And they are all I need."

The rest. He must mean the others that Ashley told me about. What was it they believed and she didn't?

"Tell me," Dr. Jordan said in a silky voice. "What exactly was it that made you so soft?"

"I'm not soft," she said after a pause. "I can finally see the difference between right and wrong."

"It was that stupid space pilot and his talk about faith and God, wasn't it? I knew I should have kept you in solitude all the way from Earth to here. Ever since then you've been acting like you've heard the voice of God or something."

Stupid space pilot. Earth to here. That was my dad. I'd never known before that it was my dad who'd had such an impact on Ashley. Neither of them had talked about it.

"No matter," Dr. Jordan continued. "All's well that ends well. And you're back under my control again."

"No. You can only brainwash a person once."

There was a loud slapping sound. Ashley drew in a sharp breath but didn't cry. *Did he just hit her?* If so, it made me so mad that I wanted to run up Dr. Jordan's face and yank out all his nose hairs. But if he found the ant-bot . . .

"You think you are so smart," Dr. Jordan said. "But when the ant-bot disappeared, I knew it had to be you or that wheelchair kid. And when I got reports about stolen food . . . I finally decided it had to be you. Somehow alive. Especially with the other kid unable to tell me a thing about the ant-bot. Now open your hand, and show me what's inside."

Everything for me swayed as Ashley lifted her hand. I was glad to be tucked under the fabric of her jumpsuit sleeve.

"Turn around," Dr. Jordan barked. "I said, 'turn around'!"

More swaying movement.

Ashley yelped.

"The transmitter!" Dr. Jordan said. He must have ripped it from her neck-plug. "I thought as much. Which tells me you *have* been using the ant-bot. So where is it?"

Silence.

"Where is it?" It sounded like Dr. Jordan had his teeth gritted.

Silence.

"I could cheerfully put you on the surface and watch the air get sucked out of you," he hissed. "That space torpedo was one of a kind. Now the ant-bot. Together that's about 30 billion dollars' worth of science. Just because suddenly you decide you have a conscience. Now tell me where it is!"

More silence.

Without warning, everything shifted violently. It felt like I was in the center of a massive earthquake.

I heard Ashley gasp. Dr. Jordan was shaking her.

"Where is it?" he shouted, losing all control of any calm in his voice. "What have you done with it?"

Ashley said nothing.

Just as suddenly the earthquake stopped.

"We're going to my office," he snarled. "If it's on you anywhere, my scanner will find it. And if it's not there, I'll find a way to make you talk."

CHAPTER 18

From the ant-bot perspective, it was a strange, strange world.

The walk from the power plant to Dr. Jordan's office wasn't a walk for me. I was a hitchhiker, hidden beneath Ashley's wristband. It felt like I was on the end of a giant pendulum, slowly swinging back and forth with the movement of her arm. Every few seconds I'd jab her skin as hard as I could, hoping she'd feel it and know I was still with her.

"Let go of my arm!" she told Dr. Jordan.

"Not likely," he said. "Don't waste your breath."

Dr. Jordan might have thought she'd wasted her breath, but I knew it was Ashley's way of telling me what was happening.

Neither of them spoke for a while after that.

This late at night, even if the scientists and tekkies weren't being held hostage in the meeting room, the dome was usually very still. The fabric of Ashley's jumpsuit muffled whatever other sounds were there, like the fans and the hum of the dome's power plant.

Altogether it was a weird, weird experience.

I might have enjoyed it, but I was desperately thinking of what to do once we got to Dr. Jordan's office.

The first thing, obviously, was to get away from Ashley.

Scanners were used to detect metal in Martian rocks. All Dr. Jordan needed to do was sweep a scanner in the air within a couple of feet of Ashley, and it would give him a beep-beep-beep confirmation of the ant-bot's location.

But how could I get away?

The jump would certainly smash the ant-bot. After all, it would be no different than taking my regular-sized robot body and leaping off a cliff over a half mile high.

I doubted I'd be able to crawl up her arm and then down her entire body to the floor in enough time.

So I'd have to depend on Ashley. Which is why I kept jabbing her wrist to remind her exactly where I was.

I shouldn't have worried for even a second.

As soon as Dr. Jordan pushed her into his office, she hit the light switch. The diffused, bluish light that made it through the fabric of her jumpsuit became totally black.

❋

"Let go!" she shouted. "Let go!"

Again my world became swirling, rocking, confusing. I had a sensation of falling, which stopped instantly a heart-beat later.

What was happening?

"You tripped me!" Ashley shouted. "I think I broke my wrist when it hit the floor."

She means that for me. To let me know the floor is nearby.

"Get up, you stupid girl."

I propelled the ant-bot forward and fell again, very briefly.

Floor!

It was still dark. I didn't know what direction I was headed, but I moved as fast as the tiny robot wheels would let me.

Seconds later the light snapped on again.

My video lens caught movement, and instinctively I spun hard right.

Something gigantic came down, thudding the floor with vibrations that wobbled me. A short gust of air blew me forward.

I'd just missed being squashed by Dr. Jordan's foot! It would have destroyed the ant-bot's computer without warning and probably scrambled my own brain circuits.

I wheeled as hard as I could toward the nearest wall, which seemed like a vertical cliff miles high. When I reached the base, I found plenty of room beneath the baseboard to hide.

I waited.

"Please don't tape my wrists to this chair," Ashley said.

"Shut your mouth. No amount of begging will stop me."

Again, Ashley was trying to help me by letting me know what was happening. She was one gutsy girl.

She and Dr. Jordan were in the center of the room.

But what could I do to help?

"Hey," Ashley said, "why is the satellite feed hooked up to your computer? Isn't that supposed to be in the director's office?"

"You have too many questions."

"Does this mean you're the only one who can contact Earth?" she asked. "That's the only satellite feed under the dome, isn't it?"

"Silence!" Dr. Jordan barked.

Ashley knew Dr. Jordan would get mad. So why had she talked about the satellite feed twice?

I answered my own question by remembering what she'd told me earlier. *"If the prisoners on Earth aren't freed within another hour, Dr. Jordan is going to execute a scientist here under the dome. He's going to send live video coverage of the execution by the satellite feed, so that the media will get it and broadcast it all across Earth. . . . He believes public pressure will make the Federation do what he wants."*

One hour left before the first execution.

Ashley was trying to tell me that the only way of reaching Earth was through the satellite feed here in this office.

Which meant if I could destroy the satellite feed, Dr. Jordan would have to wait before executing anyone.

But that was a big, big if for a small, small ant-bot. . . .

CHAPTER 19

I followed the base of the wall at full speed, reached a corner, and kept going as fast as I could in the new direction.

In a full-sized body, it would have only taken three steps to reach the desk on the other side of Dr. Jordan's office. In the ant-bot, it seemed like a half mile. By the time I completed the journey, Dr. Jordan had returned with the scanner to search Ashley.

Although from my perspective it was much too far to see into the middle of the room, I knew the scanner was not much different than the metal detector wands I'd seen in movies.

"After this," I heard Ashley ask, "what next? How do you get back to Earth? How do you know you won't be arrested?"

Computer cables hung loosely from the desk, falling in loose coils on the floor. To me the cables looked like massive tree trunks, with the surface rough enough for me to climb them. So I reached up with one of the ant-bot's tiny arms and began climbing.

"How are you going to get away with this?" Ashley persisted. "I thought you were much smarter."

Arm over arm, I pulled myself upward. Rawling had once trained me for this in my regular-sized robot.

I guessed Ashley was asking Dr. Jordan the questions to distract him. She didn't know, of course, what I was doing, but I'm sure she wanted to delay him.

"I mean," she continued, "you can't stay on Mars forever. And you'll be arrested as soon as you step off the shuttle."

I kept climbing. I didn't expect Dr. Jordan to respond.

But he did. I guessed he was probably too vain to want a girl Ashley's age to think he was stupid.

"There's plenty of places I can hide on the Moon-base," he said. "And that's where the shuttle will make an unexpected stop. From the moon, I can take any number of daily flights back down to Earth."

The Moon-base, I thought. It had been established 10 years before the Mars Project. With short shuttles making it easy to deliver supplies and work parties, it now covered the size of a city, while the base on Mars was still little more than the original dome.

I heard the beep-beep-beep of the scanner. I was three-quarters of the way up the cable.

"Aha," Dr. Jordan said. "Hidden in your hair!"

"That's a hair clip," Ashley said. "I can save you the trouble. I don't have the ant-bot."

"Nice try," he replied.

I reached the top of the cable. The ant-bot wasn't tired, of course, because robots never tired. They ran until the power pack was depleted. I hoped that either a robot this small was very efficient or that Ashley had charged the power pack recently.

"Told you," Ashley said. "Hair clip."

That let me imagine the scene in the center of the room.

If her arms were taped to the armrest of a chair, Dr. Jordan would be leaning over her, disappointed to find only a hair clip.

I scurried across the desk in the shadow of the computer. It was like walking along the bottom of a massive building.

The scanner beeped again.

"Another hair clip," Ashley said.

I ran beneath the shell of the computer. It was much dimmer, but I could look up and get enough light through the tiny cooling vents. There was a gap in the underside of the computer shell. It would allow me to climb into the computer, except the underside was too high for me to reach. Like a person standing beneath a ceiling.

And even if I got in there, what could I do to short-circuit it?

That's when I realized I had asked exactly the right question.

Short-circuit.

Safely hidden, I surveyed the top of Dr. Jordan's desk.

There was a pen, looking like a log to me.

And a paper clip.

The pen was almost right beside the computer. I scurried out and pushed one end. I felt very much like an ant as half of the pen slowly rolled beneath the computer.

"How do you know that someone else didn't take the ant-bot?" Ashley asked from the center of the room, her voice echoing weirdly. "Because I can tell you that I don't have it."

"No one else but you or the wheelchair kid can use it."

"What if someone decided to use it as proof of the existence of your secret military program? What if the right people on Earth somehow found out that you've taken billions and billions from government programs?"

I heard the sound of a slap.

"Is that what you do when you don't have a good answer?" Ashley asked. "Hit people? Like that proves you right?"

Ashley could only be doing this to distract him. Maybe she'd seen over his shoulder and noticed my little movements on the desk. If that was true, I didn't have much time. I scrambled back from the edge of the bottom of the computer and went for the paper clip. I wrestled with it and managed to drag it under the computer.

"Tell me where you've hidden Project 3," Dr. Jordan hissed.

I lifted the paper clip, balancing it on end. Twice it nearly fell. But I managed to push it up into the gap. It leaned against the edge of the gap, and I was able to climb onto the pen. One big shove and the paper clip fell into the base of the computer.

"There's nothing you can do to me," Ashley said with determined defiance.

"Really?" Dr. Jordan asked.

With one hand I was able to grab the edge of the gap and pull myself up. With the other hand I pushed and let the ant-bot topple inside. I was now in the guts of the computer, armed with a paper clip.

I froze as I heard Dr. Jordan's next words.

"Fine," he said to Ashley. "You'll talk when I bring the wheelchair kid in here and show you how painful I can make life for him."

"Tyce? How can you hurt Tyce?"

I frantically wrestled the paper clip.

"Very easily. See you in a minute." He laughed cruelly. "Sit tight while I'm gone."

I heard the door shut behind him.

"Tyce?" Ashley called out frantically a few seconds later. "Tyce. Did you hear that? You need to leave the ant-bot!"

I was too busy with the paper clip to answer.

CHAPTER 20

I opened my eyes in the darkness of the storage room.

How long before Dr. Jordan arrives from his office on the other side of the dome?

I didn't waste any time. First I reached behind me and disconnected the transmitter from my neck. I dropped it down the back of my jumpsuit again. All I could do was hope Dr. Jordan didn't decide to search me again. But there was no point in trying to dump it. Without the transmitter, Ashley and I had no chance at all.

Seconds later the door opened without warning.

It was Dr. Jordan. With the security guard beside him.

"Take him," Dr. Jordan commanded. "And follow me to my office."

❈

"It's very simple, Ashley." Dr. Jordan paced back and forth in front of both of us. He had taken me into his office and sent the security guard back to help watch the other hostages. Ashley was still in her chair, taped by the arms to the armrests. I was in my wheelchair, helpless, as always. "You tell me where you've hidden Project 3, or your friend Tyce becomes the first hostage to be executed."

Dr. Jordan pointed at the satellite feed attached to his computer. "It will make for a spectacular news story, don't you think? People will be riveted to their 3-D sets for television history. He's young, he's in a wheelchair, and not only was he the first person born on Mars, he'll be the first to die on Mars."

Ashley turned her head and stared at me. Her face twisted with horror and dread.

"No, Ashley," I said. "You can't tell him."

"Best of all, Ashley," Dr. Jordan continued, "you'll be right here watching it live."

Dr. Jordan moved to his desk and picked up a neuron gun. He pointed it at my wrist, which rested on the armrest of my wheelchair.

Then he smiled and squeezed the trigger.

There was no sound, nothing for the eye to see. But the electrical impulses hit me instantly, disabling the nerve endings of my left wrist and hand.

I couldn't help myself. I lifted my other arm and yelled. My left hand and wrist hung uselessly.

"How was that?" Dr. Jordan asked Ashley. "Would you like to see more?"

"Please don't shoot him again," I heard Ashley beg above the pain that seemed to roar in my ears. "Project 3 is in the top drawer of your desk."

I lifted my head as if it had been jerked by a puppet string. I stared at her in shock that she'd told him. The last thing I'd done with the ant-bot before waking in my own body was scurry from the computer to the edge of the desk to drop in that drawer. *Was she betraying me again?*

"You're lying to me," Dr. Jordan told her.

"No, I'm not. Your own office is the last place in the world you'd look."

Slowly Dr. Jordan moved to his desk. He opened the drawer and bent over to see better. A second later he plucked something out and balanced it on his palm. He looked at it against the light.

"It really *is* the ant-bot," he said, grinning. "Clever. Very clever. Too bad you didn't remain one of us."

"You've got what you want," Ashley said. "At least let us join his mom and dad now."

Dr. Jordan's grin widened. "Hardly. It's time for Tyce's execution. And if they don't release the prisoners on Earth, a half hour later you'll follow. After all, why waste good scientists and tekkies when I can get rid of the two who have made my life the most miserable over the past week?"

"No!" Ashley shouted. "I told you where to find what you wanted. You have to—"

She stopped shouting as Dr. Jordan pointed the neuron gun at her.

"That's better," he said. "Noise gives me such a headache."

He walked back to the desk again. Before facing the computer and satellite feed, he spoke to me one more time.

"Time to make you a television star, Tyce. It will be a performance to die for."

CHAPTER 21

Normally the person contacting Earth sat in a chair in front of the satellite feed, a simple black box with a small video lens.

But Dr. Jordan pushed the chair aside, returned for me, and pushed my wheelchair forward until I was a couple of feet away, staring directly into the eye of the camera.

"This will be so simple," he said. "You're a sitting duck. Perfect height to catch all the expressions on your face."

"I feel sorry for you," I said.

It caught him off guard. *"You* feel sorry for *me?"*

"You think you're winning, but in the end you're going to die too. Only you'll have reason to be afraid of dying."

During the oxygen crisis, I'd finally been able to believe the most important thing a person can learn. Dying doesn't mean the end, so dying isn't the worst thing that can happen to a person. Not when God is waiting.

He sneered. "Spare me that faith nonsense. No one has power over me. I'll do what I want for as long as I want. And that will last for years and years after you've turned to dust."

Dr. Jordan turned his back on me. He had no reason to

worry that I could do anything. Not from my wheelchair. Not unless he fell into my lap.

I had to twist my head to watch him step up to his computer. The satellite feed ran through a program on the computer. If the computer started properly, I truly was dead. And I knew I'd need God's help through the last moments of neuron gun torture.

But if the computer wouldn't operate . . .

He snapped on the power button. I was hoping for a sizzle or pop, hoping the paper clip I'd struggled to lay across the power relay inside the computer box would short-circuit the system.

And I got far more than I hoped for.

Instead of a sizzle or pop, the entire computer screen exploded, sending a surge of blue light toward Dr. Jordan's stomach!

I think it was more the surprise than the electrical surge that threw him back.

He staggered toward me with a small yelp. He bumped into my wheelchair and began to fall.

Right across my lap!

What I wanted to do was push forward and fall out of my wheelchair and roll on top of him and somehow wrestle with him until he gave up.

But his weight changed that.

He'd locked the brakes on my wheelchair and, braced from going backward, it flipped forward with his weight. Because I was trying to push forward too, it gave extra force.

Dr. Jordan's head hit the edge of the desk with a sickening thump.

He tumbled to the floor, groaned once as he flopped a few times, then collapsed completely.

Unconscious.

"His neuron gun," Ashley said after a second of silent disbelief. "Can you get it from him?"

I, too, stared in disbelief. "Won't work for me," I answered. "Each gun is matched to the fingerprints programmed into it."

"We've got to do something. Fast. He could wake up any second."

I stared at Dr. Jordan for another couple of seconds. His glasses had fallen from his face.

"Can you slide your chair this way?" I asked Ashley. "I think I have an idea."

CHAPTER 22

Ten minutes later, Blaine Steven walked into Dr. Jordan's office.

I couldn't see him. I could only hear his first words to Dr. Jordan. His voice was muffled to me. "I came as soon as possible. What is—"

I knew why he'd stopped in surprise, because I could picture what he saw.

Ashley was standing near the computer with the busted screen. I was slumped in my wheelchair, my head down, in the robot activation zone of concentration, with the transmitter connected to my neck-plug. And Dr. Jordan sat in the chair where Ashley had been taped to the armrest. Only now Dr. Jordan was the one whose wrists were taped in place, his right hand holding the neuron gun, pointed at the doorway.

"Dr. Jordan!" Blaine Steven said. "Your face!" There was a pause. "Your nose!"

I could picture, too, exactly how it appeared to Blaine Steven. Dr. Jordan's nose had been duct-taped shut. That way he couldn't sneeze or snort out a blast of air. Otherwise, the ant-bot would be gone, and there would be no way to force Dr. Jordan to do as he'd been told.

I waited for him to follow the first step of our instructions.

A loud, angry yell reached me.

Step 1. Hit Blaine in the legs with the neuron gun. Right on schedule.

"Shut up," Dr. Jordan told Blaine Steven. Dr. Jordan's voice was loud to me. Very loud. "And do exactly as I say. Ashley is going to tape your hands together. Let her do it, or I'll be forced to fire another shot."

"That's a . . . that's a . . ."

"Yes," Dr. Jordan told Blaine Steven. "It's a neuron gun."

"But, but . . ."

I wasn't surprised Blaine Steven sounded muffled to me or Dr. Jordan's voice was loud and echoed weirdly. I was, after all, in Dr. Jordan's sinus passage.

Seconds later I heard Ashley. "It's done, Tyce. He's taped. Wrists and ankles."

Good. Dr. Jordan was taped in his chair. Blaine Steven was sitting on the floor, also taped and helpless. They couldn't do anything to Ashley now.

"Give me the computer code that disables all the neuron guns," Dr. Jordan said. "If you do, I'll send Ashley to your office, where she'll enter the code. And then you'll be safe."

"Have you lost your mind?" came Blaine Steven's voice. I imagined his face growing red with rage underneath his thick gray hair.

"No," Dr. Jordan said. "Give me the code, or I'll have to shoot again."

"Jordan," Blaine Steven said, "if I disable your gun, all

the neuron guns under the dome will be disabled. What's gotten into you?"

Ashley's giggle reached me too. "That's a better question than you know."

If the ant-bot robot body had been capable of giggling, I'd have done it too.

Ashley continued to speak. "Tyce, give Dr. Jordan a reminder of why he should obey us."

I did. Reaching out a robot arm, I pounded once inside the darkness.

Dr. Jordan moaned.

⚛

While Dr. Jordan had been unconscious, Ashley had moved her chair close enough to me so I could rip the tape off her wrists. I'd helped her as much as I could to move him into the chair, and she had quickly taped Dr. Jordan's wrists together, then taken the ant-bot and placed it on his upper lip.

I'd plugged in with the mini-transmitter and, in control of the ant-bot, had gone straight up Dr. Jordan's nose, past the nose hairs that seemed like fence posts. Then Ashley had taped his nose so that he couldn't blow me out.

Let me be the first to say that the inside of someone's nose is as gooey and slimy as you can imagine. But I hadn't been able to think of anything nearly as effective. I'd traveled as far up his nose as possible, then waited for him to wake.

Minutes later, when he finally grunted himself back to consciousness, Ashley had informed him of his situation. From inside the nasal passage, the ant-bot audio sensors had let me hear her threaten him.

"It's very elementary, Dr. Jordan. If the ant-bot goes up

any farther, it can penetrate your brain. You don't want that, do you? Tyce, let him know you've got the ant-bot in there."

That's when I'd done it the first time. Begun hammering the sensitive tissue of his sinus passage with both robot arms. He'd understood the message.

Then Ashley had given him the rest of his instructions, beginning with a call to bring in Blaine Steven.

⚛

It took only one hit on the inside of his nasal passage to convince Dr. Jordan he needed to follow the rest of the instructions.

I heard another yelp. This one from Blaine Steven again. As instructed earlier, Dr. Jordan must have shot him in the shoulder. Briefly I felt sorry for Blaine Steven. I knew what that felt like.

"Now do you understand I'm serious?" I heard Dr. Jordan ask. "Give me the code to disable the guns."

"Yes! Yes!" Blaine Steven whined. "I understand. You can have the code."

He gave us the right one, the first time.

Which would make the next part a lot easier.

CHAPTER 23

"Hello," I said to Dad. "Can you hear me?"

His head spun up and down and side to side, just like I'd done when I'd first heard the ant-bot's voice. I wished I could see the expression on his face. But I was controlling the ant-bot, perched on his shoulder, lighter than a fly. And with only two lights burning in the entire large meeting room, I was nearly invisible on his jumpsuit. I was far too close to see his face.

"Can you hear me?" I repeated. From Dr. Jordan's office, it had taken a half hour to reach the meeting room with the ant-bot. I'd gotten lost twice. Going down corridors that seem two miles wide is a confusing thing.

"I can hear you," he whispered with hesitation. "Unless I'm losing my mind. But who are *you?*"

In any other situation, I'd have been tempted to have fun with this. But I resisted. I was certain the hostages would all be safe soon enough, but I knew too well that Rawling was still stuck under tons of rock. The sooner the scientists and tekkies took control of the dome, the sooner the rescue attempt could begin.

"The guards can't stop you now," I said. "Their guns won't work."

Again, Dad's head spun from side to side. "Is this some ventriloquist joke? Who's playing games?"

"Dad," I said, "it's Tyce. Really. I'd tell you where I am, but I'm afraid you'd knock me off as you look for me."

"Tyce?" he asked. "Tyce?"

Before I could answer, Mom's voice interrupted. "Honey, quit mumbling. You'll wake the others around us."

Dad said nothing. I could guess what was going through his mind. If he told Mom he was answering some voice that came to him from the darkness, she'd think he'd suddenly gone crazy.

"I'm real," I told Dad, and then I used the words he always said to me. "Trust me."

"Did you hear that?" he asked Mom quickly. "It's a voice!"

"You're dreaming, honey," she said. "Go back to sleep." She patted his back and nearly knocked me off his shoulder.

Time to get serious, before the ant-bot was hurt.

"I know this is hard to believe, but it *is* Tyce," I said. I needed to come up with something he knew only I could know. "The last time we spoke, I was trying to feed you live video from the cave-in."

There was a pause, and then, "Tyce?"

"Dad, you've got to trust me. The neuron guns won't fire anymore. Wake everyone up. It's 200 of you against six of them. They don't have a chance. Then come and get me from Dr. Jordan's office."

Dad groaned. "How can I believe a voice in the dark?"

"It's Project 3, Dad. A miniaturized robot called an *ant-*

bot. Don't move. I'll pinch your neck to show you this is real."

I did.

He laughed in the darkness. "Tyce!"

"Two hundred against six, Dad," I said one more time. "All you need to do is walk up there and ask one of the guards to shoot you. When everybody sees that his gun doesn't work, the fight will be over."

And that was it.

Except for the cave-in.

CHAPTER 24

During the first crisis that hit the dome, Mom asked me to keep a diary so that Earth people would know what it was like to live on Mars. Even though we survived the oxygen-level disaster, Mom insisted I keep writing about what happens on Mars. She has a good point—no one else in the solar system can say they grew up on this planet. At least not yet. And she says that my diaries will at least let me look back when I'm an old man and remember everything a lot easier.

Even though she's right, there have been times I complained to Mom about writing my diary entries. I'd much rather be up at the telescope or working with the robot bodies.

I've decided, though, that I'll never complain again.

Here I am, parked in front of my computer, when only 24 hours earlier I was a prisoner in a storage room, afraid of what might happen to me and my parents and the other scientists under the dome, and especially worried about the cave-in.

It's great to be safe. With my biggest problem being what words to put on a blank computer screen. I could be there again, in front of the piled-up rocks of the cave-in, frantically scared that once we dug through, we would find Rawling and the other three dead.

I closed my eyes and thought about what it was like to be there. When I was ready, I began to type my next diary entry.

09.24.2039

If the rescue team had been forced to depend on tekkies in space suits, the oxygen and water of the men trapped by all that rock would have run out long before anyone could have reached them.

Instead, it became the Mars Project's best argument for the use of robot bodies controlled by humans like me or Ashley.

We began the rescue attempt early in the morning after the scientists and tekkies had locked up Steven, Jordan, and the guards. The temperature beneath the jet-black Martian sky had dropped to -150° Fahrenheit. Wind had picked up, making it even colder.

But Ashley and I were back in the dome, miles away, warm and comfortable and relaxed. Relaxed, except for our minds. Connected by the remotes to our robot bodies, we were concentrating as hard as if we were in a marathon video game. And what was better, we were working at it together.

At our direction, all those miles away from the dome, the robot bodies picked up rocks and threw them backward far faster than any human could work. We were helped by two things. First, the robots could lift rocks six times heavier than any Olympic weight lifter. And second, because of the reduced gravity on Mars, even the heaviest of rocks were within the load capabilities of the robots. And, unlike human bodies, the robots didn't get tired. A platform buggy stood nearby, with tekkies ready to replace the robot batteries.

The robots worked out there, side by side, for 15 hours straight, taking breaks only when Ashley and I got too tired to concentrate.

And in the 16th hour we broke through.

Rawling and the other three were in a deep pocket of space, close to their last breaths of oxygen.

Dad tells us that while Ashley and I were handling the robots, the dramatic rescue attempt was captured live on video and transmitted to Earth media sources. All across the Earth, people watched as Rawling got to his feet and hugged my robot.

Dad says that one image was enough to earn renewed support for the Mars Project and for the budget it would take to develop the robot bodies even more.

Dr. Jordan and Blaine Steven never did get their chance for worldwide attention, but the robots did.

And I have to admit, I liked that!

EPILOGUE

"It was a setup from the beginning," Rawling McTigre said, scratching his short, dark hair that was streaked with gray. "The bombs were in one of the packs. If we hadn't set them against the side of the cave before going in deeper, we would have died instantly."

Rawling and I sat on the upper floor of the dome, at the telescope. It was good to see him healthy after wondering if I'd ever see him alive again.

"Dr. Jordan wanted you out of the dome before he began his takeover."

"Exactly," Rawling said. "I should have been suspicious when he insisted that the search needed a medical person. But his position gave him even more authority than dome director. . . ."

I stared upward through the dome at the incredibly black sky of a Martian night. "You won't have to worry about him anymore, huh?"

"Wrong, Tyce."

He said it so sharply that I snapped my head back.

"Think about it. He nearly engineered civil war back on Earth. It's not something he could do without help. And then there are the others you've told me about. Tomorrow we're going to learn everything we can from Ashley. I think there's a lot more to worry about."

He was right. I had plenty of questions too. Because of the cave-in rescue operation—with both Ashley and me controlling the big robots to help move rock—things had been too frantic for me to ask her about anything. Including how she'd survived the Hammerhead space torpedo crash.

Tomorrow. Not only would we talk to Ashley, but tomorrow marked the last day I'd see my dad for three years. Tomorrow night the shuttle headed back to Earth. With Blaine Steven and Dr. Jordan along as prisoners.

"Tyce?" Rawling broke into my thoughts. "Look."

He pointed. I didn't need the telescope to know what it was.

Earth.

"Must be strange," I said. "Seeing it hang there night after night, with all your memories of growing up there."

Rawling laughed. "No more strange than seeing it hang there night after night, being the only human in history never to have spent any time there."

"Yeah," I said softly, "it is strange."

"Probably be even more strange seeing it for the first time."

"Yeah," I said, "it would be."

"Not *would,* Tyce. *Will.*"

I wasn't sure I understood. "It *will* be strange to see it for the first time?"

Rawling patted my shoulder. "Tomorrow night. You and Ashley will be on the ship with your dad."

"What!"

"For the Mars Project to survive, Tyce, we need a lot of questions answered. And Mars isn't the place to find those answers. You will go, won't you? I've already talked with your parents about it, and even your mom agrees that she wants you to go."

I hardly heard him.

I was staring at that ball of white and blue, 50 million miles away.

Earth.

DOES GOD SPEAK TO PEOPLE?

I have to admit, I'm a lot like Tyce Sanders when it comes to writing. While I like telling stories and I *really* like to finish writing a book, I find the process itself difficult. Like Tyce, there are a lot of other things I'd prefer to do than face a blank computer screen.

However, I found one part of this book a lot of fun to write. It's the part where Tyce thinks God is speaking to him, like a voice out of thin air.

I was even tempted to have Ashley tell him more things to mess his mind completely. *Tyce, do your homework. Tyce, stop picking your nose when you think nobody's looking.* Stuff like that.

But because I look at the world through both a scientific and faith perspective, I realize how important the question really is. *Does God speak to people?*

In one way, he certainly has. The Bible is God's book, with his message to us. It gives us guidelines for how to live life best and points us to the one way we can reach God through faith.

But does he really *speak* to people? Today? In our own lives?

I believe yes.

Perhaps not with an actual voice.

But through our conscience, through quiet moments when we suddenly understand something that wasn't clear before, through the gentle instruction from other people who know him well.

But what many people struggle with is that the ways God speaks to us can't often be proven. As Tyce says in this book, "Having faith in God means you decide to trust him, even when you can't see the outcome. Since scientists are used to seeing results and proof, and since it's scientifically impossible to prove God exists, some of them want to think that the only things that exist are the things you can measure."

Why do so many scientists see a conflict between science (data that can be proven by A + B = C) and faith (something you feel inside your heart and believe with your mind, but can't hear, taste, or touch)? It's true that believing in God means taking a leap of faith. But believing in God isn't totally illogical, as some people believe.

You see, humans are not just made of body and mind. We are capable of love. Of loneliness. Of longing. Things that can't be measured or found during a medical examination. Things that also point to the existence of a soul.

When God speaks to us, I believe he speaks to our souls.

As Tyce realized in this book, we just have to find those quiet moments where we can hear him. We have to learn to listen.

ABOUT THE AUTHOR

Sigmund Brouwer, his wife, recording artist Cindy Morgan, and their daughter split living between Red Deer, Alberta, Canada, and Nashville, Tennessee. He has written several series of juvenile fiction and eight novels. Sigmund loves sports and plays golf and hockey. He also enjoys visiting schools to talk about books. He welcomes visitors to his Web site at www.coolreading.com, where he and a bunch of other authors like to hang out in cyberspace.

MARS
DIARIES

are you ready?

Set in an experimental community on Mars in the year 2039, the Mars Diaries feature 14-year-old virtual-reality specialist Tyce Sanders. Life on the red planet is not always easy, but it is definitely exciting. As Tyce explores his strange surroundings, he also finds that the mysteries of the planet point to his greatest discovery—a new relationship with God.

MISSION 1: OXYGEN LEVEL ZERO
Can Tyce stop the oxygen leak in time?

MISSION 2: ALIEN PURSUIT
What attacked the tekkie in the lab?

MISSION 3: TIME BOMB
What mystery is uncovered by the quake?

MISSION 4: HAMMERHEAD
Will the comet crash on Earth, destroying all life?

MISSION 5: SOLE SURVIVOR
Will a hostile takeover destroy the Mars Project?

MISSION 6 COMING SPRING 2001
Discover the latest news about the Mars Diaries.
Visit www.marsdiaries.com